THE RAM OF GOD

AND OTHER STORIES

THE RAM OF GOD
AND OTHER STORIES

JOHN B. KEANE

THE MERCIER PRESS

The Mercier Press
PO Box No. 5, 5 French Church Street, Cork
24 Lower Abbey Street, Dublin 1

© John B. Keane 1991

First published 1992
ISBN 1 85635 01 7 7

A CIP record of this book is available from the British Library.

Printed in Ireland by Colour Books Ltd.

Contents

The Ram of God

From time to time readers ask me about characters from the essays and stories I have written over the years. Without doubt the greater number of queries concern a man who was affectionately known as the Ram of God. He is dead now the poor fellow and so are all his relations which is sad in one way but good in the sense that we are now free to discuss the short career of the Ram in question.

It was said of him that he sired countless offspring in the Stacks Mountains of my native North Kerry before finally departing to the state of Montana where he expired a few short years ago. It would not matter much if he had taken the precaution or had the common decency, as they say, to marry before siring but this was not the poor fellow's way.

The Ram was the youngest son of a small farmer. For the want of something more fitting he was sent off at the tender age of eighteen to become a priest. Two years before he was to become ordained, however, he discovered that he had no vocation so he returned shamefacedly to his home in the Stacks.

In his heyday, from the beginning to the end of the Second World War, he was without peer in the holy art of seduction. He never broke hearts, however. He made his intentions clear from the outset. There was never a slow waltzer or a cheek to cheek foxtrotter like him. His favourite song was:

Say little hen!
When, when, when
Will you lay me an egg for my tea?

His favourite book was *Robinson Crusoe* and his favourite type of woman was red-haired. Oddly enough he was less successful with redheads than with blondes or brunettes.

For some reason best known to himself he always most assiduously avoided visiting Dan Paddy Andy's famous dance hall at the Cross of Renagown but one night in a pub in Tralee he announced that it was his intention to pay a call there. He was never to fulfil his promise. When Dan heard that the Ram of God was about to descend upon the innocent and sheltered females of Renagown and its hinterland he made one of his most memorable announcements from a musician's butterbox in his dance hall: 'If the Ram of God makes the mistake of coming here,' he warned, 'he'll go home a wether.'

The Ram of God was so-called because of the fact that he spent such a long time studying for the priesthood and because of his excessive and unseemly interest in the opposite sex. The fact that he flourished in that prohibitive clime and time sets him apart.

'I had nothin' agin' the poor hoor personally,' Dan Paddy once was heard to say, 'and his failing was the failing of many but I had my flock to look out for and I wasn't going to let him loose in Renagown.'

After helping out on the family farm for the period of the war years the Ram hightailed it to Leicester City and afterwards to Montana where he set up a calf-fattening station some miles to the south-east of the town of Goose Creek. Very soon he was chasing females like nobody's business but this time the parents of his victims were gun-totin', ornery side-winders who didn't take too kindly to strangers molesting their womenfolk.

With more than three score of shotgun pellets embedded in his buttocks he fled to New York where he worked as a barman until his demise a few years ago. In New York where all kinds of loose females are said to reside he had no problem with parents or brothers so we must presume that he did not change his ways.

In life, according to those who knew him, he was a most agreeable fellow, a stout friend and a strong ally provided he was segregated from the wives and daughters of his associates.

I came across an old Stacks Mountains man recently in the town of Tralee who suggested to me that a monument should be erected to the Ram or some sort of plaque fastened to one of the outer walls of the crumbling ruin where he first saw the light. *Birthplace of the Ram of God* was the inscription suggested by the old man.

Well that's the Ram's tale for those who are interested. Undoubtedly he was a man before his time. I wonder if he's fondly thought of in Goose Creek, Montana, or if he's remembered more for the quality of his veal than his romantic exploits?

Misdirected Drops

The other night, gazing out my window at the naked moon as she cast her pale beams all around I saw the strangest sight of my entire life. I thought until then that I had seen everything that the stage of night, after the pubs close, presents for the titillation of humanity but, like Horatio, I was to learn that there are more things in heaven and earth than are dealt with in my philosophy.

Below me stood a middle-aged man with a head like an Airedale terrier. He stood blissfully with his legs apart, simulating the stance of a casual if drunken piddler. I presumed that he was divesting himself of the excess waters processed so painstakingly by his heavily-taxed kidneys. His pose was perfect for this age-old ritualistic exercise and to the ordinary passer-by it would certainly seem that he was in the throes of bladderly relief.

Yet there was no physical evidence of kidney-confected showerings, no sound of cascading droplets, nothing whatsoever to indicate that this most natural of undertakings was in progress. He stood there, the very epitome of exalted rapture. I knew the fellow well. He was and is a great frequenter of pubs so that nature could be expected to take advantage of him occasionally under the most unfavourable of circumstances. Those of us who indulge in the occasional pint or two will sympathise with him.

Meanwhile people were passing to and fro as the

pubs discharged the last of their patrons. Little notice was taken of this nocturnal mimer. As far as the passers-by were concerned he was the genuine article. The pose was right and that was what mattered. In no time at all he had the street to himself save for the presence of a venerable canine who happened to be a resident of the locality.

Overhead the great huntress of the heavens shone serenely on dog and man. One by one the lights in the residences of the conjoining thoroughfares were doused and from a darkened doorway a tomcat mewed querulously in the hope that a neighbourhood pussy might hear. A child cried and was lovingly silenced as its lamentations were transformed into happy chortlings and thence to slumber. From far away came the pitiful brayings of a romance-starved jackass whilst overhead a rumbling, grumbling jet conveyed its cargo of passengers through the star-filled heavens and still our friend retained his stance and discharged his obligations to brain and bladder.

It seemed that he would spend the entire night in the same happy position but then suddenly he buttoned imaginary flies as though he had been reminded of an important appointment. He stood for a moment looking up and down the street not certain from where he had come or to where he was bound. He moved slowly and then the evidence was revealed as the water trickled from inside his trousers on to the street. It then dawned on the poor fellow that he had wet his trousers.

He walked in that lopsided fashion so common to trousers-wetters everywhere. Judging from the amount of time he spent relieving himself the trousers must have been very wet indeed. I watched this inexquisite

11

picture of human folly as he endeavoured to walk homewards where he would immediately divest himself of the offensive garment. It took him a long time to travel the fifty or so yards where he would be obliged to cross the road. So ungainly and cumbersome was his gait that a passing motorist hooted him to get on with it. He crossed over and I saw him no more. I had not seen the exercise he performed executed previously although I am pretty sure that there must have been countless examples since trousers were first worn by man.

The moon shone elegantly the while, lofty and disdainful, witness to another example of man's unending fallibility. Unencumbered by trousers the resident canine relieved himself against the corner, looked with some perplexity at the moon and went off about his business. I retired from the window, glad that I had witnessed this slight but deviant farce at no charge to myself or the taxpayer.

Fear

I am convinced that fear is the only malady that man will never conquer. By degrees, slowly and painfully, disease after incurable disease is being taken on and overcome by man's persistent efforts. It is man who mostly manufactures fear. We can elude the wild beast, destroy him if necessary. We can survive the elements at their worst by taking precautions. There are disasters from time to time but only because man has persistently under-estimated the elements.

But where does fear begin? For me, it began in the school, the very place where it was not supposed to begin and it didn't begin with teachers. It began with garsúns a little older than myself. A year is an awful difference in a garsún. Often, when there is such a difference between two small boys, it is much the same as a confrontation between a lightweight and a heavyweight. All other things being equal, the boy with the year advantage is a cast-iron certainty to win out. I was afraid of bullies at school and they were afraid too of bigger boys or of brutality in their homes and so forth and so on *ad infinitum*.

Two distinct advantages in any confrontation between schoolboys were squints and scars. Let the boy with the squint be a disaster as a pugilist he had, nevertheless, the edge on his opponent if he played his cards right. He could look at him in the eye with the most advantageous consequences because, when confronted with a squint, the chap at the receiving end hasn't an earthly from what quarter the attack is about to be mounted or whether the left or right hand is going to be deployed as a decoy.

Often too, a chap with a squint would seem to be looking over the shoulder of his opponent giving the impression that aid might be forthcoming from that quarter in the event of emergency. In my time I was frequently confronted by a squint. I would sooner face a chap twice my size than one with a squint.

A scar, however, was another kettle of fish. A chap with a scar on his face was rarely called upon to defend himself. The scar was better than a weapon to him. Better still, it had the value of a battle citation, and the bigger the better. In my time I have seen garsúns with scars swagger through crowds of bully-boys who would normally interrogate every innocent who passed their way. The bully-boys would always make way for the scarred. There would be nudgings and eggings-on by ringleaders but nobody wanted to find out if the scar had been earned in combat or by accident. The result was that the scarred veteran of six or seven had a right-of-way wherever he went.

The same applied to a chap with a lame leg or a crutch. However, one needed to be a very good actor to get away with a lame leg and if one presented a lame leg without a scratch or a swelling or some other outward sign of injury, the jig was up. Bandages didn't always work either. Bandages could be peeled off by the bully-boy and God help the invalid if there were no marks or blood-stains underneath.

Of course, all these subterfuges were created by fear. The innocent quail will pretend to be possessed of a broken wing when danger threatens her young. She will divert the passer-by or the overly-curious by giving the impression that her wing is really broken. Man is different. He uses subterfuge to save his own skin, most of the time.

Spectacles were also a great subterfuge. A young chap, when offered to fight against his will, would take off his glasses and pretend he couldn't see. He would, instead, volunteer to wrestle, wrestling not being a very dangerous exercise so long as the victim allowed himself to be pinned to the ground.

Fear was at the back of it all, mostly fear of what might happen. How's that Shakespeare puts it in *Julius Caesar*:

> *Cowards die many times before their deaths;*
> *The valiant never taste of death but once.*

Yes, indeed, as I said at the beginning, there is no known antidote for fear unless one faces up to it. This is not always wise because it is how orphans and widows come into being.

Fear is a malady but it need not be that bad a malady like miserliness or grandeur. Take it away and we are without the body's last line of defence. A modicum of fear is necessary as well as good. It brings us prudence which is another name for our guardian angel.

Without a leavening of fear most people would be unbearable. On top of that, the human race would annihilate itself in no time at all because without fear we would be at each other's throats morning, noon and night. We would be without respect for each other and courage, one of man's finest possessions, would be absolutely worthless.

So maybe it's a good thing that we have cowards

15

and that they die many times before their deaths. Fear, I believe, is one of the most essential ingredients in man's make-up.

When I was young I often heard it said of a man that he was without fear. This could not have been true. The man in question, I am certain, was merely better at concealing fear than most men. He was possessed of fear without doubt but he always gave the impression that he was not and this is a great sign of a man. He can carry the day by keeping his cool. We are all, give or take a taste, possessed of the same leavening of fear but it is how we handle that fear that distinguishes us from the coward and this is the very essence of our treatise here today.

I remember after a football game, many years ago, several of us players who had remained behind in the village were surrounded by a hostile mob as we were about to leave. Our enemies, egged on by a well-known blackguard, were whipping themselves into a frenzy and it looked as if we faced a terrible beating. Then one of our party spoke in low tones which only we could hear. He was a half-back.

'Don't give it to say to the hoors,' said he, 'that we're afraid of them. Stand fast now and we'll get out of this no bother.'

So saying, he leaped forward in front of the egger-on and challenged him to single combat. He crumpled and suddenly the danger which threatened had evaporated and we were allowed to leave the village in peace.

Our half-back, as we all knew well, was not exactly the bravest man in the world. In fact he always maintained that he was cowardly.

'I'm windy,' he used to say, 'but don't tell me because I already know it.'

Yet he concealed his fear and succeeded in averting a potentially nasty situation. How did he bring himself to do it?

Very simple. He knew exactly how little courage he had but, little as that was, it was more than the amount possessed by the egger-on. In fact, I doubt if he had any courage at all. Men with courage don't behave the way he behaved. Only men with too little courage and too much fear behave in such a fashion.

Now I have to leave you for I am also possessed of a fear and it is a fear common to all writers. It is the fear of boring his readers, a crime of which every writer stands terrified of being convicted.

Is Cork Sinking?

This summer a man I had never seen before entered the premises and declared to all and sundry that Cork was sinking. Having made the announcement he called for a small Paddy and a pint of stout.

There was no immediate reaction to this outrageous revelation. You must wait awhile for an appropriate response when you suddenly tell a bar full of Kerrymen that Cork is sinking. It isn't that they don't care, it is simply that they are slow to react to news, be that news good or bad.

Those with poor hearing endeavoured to ascertain if the intruder had really said that Cork was sinking.

'About time,' said one old gentleman when it was confirmed for him that Ireland's largest county was soon to be submerged for all time.

'And I'll tell you something else,' said the stranger who made the announcement, 'when Cork sinks Kerry will sink with it because the larger county will drag it down.'

'That means so,' said a bespectacled garsún who happened to be in the company of his parents, 'that all the other counties will sink as well because Kerry and Cork together are so heavy that they will bring down Limerick. That's three counties down and the weight of the three will bring down Clare and Tipperary.'

'Exactly,' said the Corkman, 'and Waterford and Kilkenny, then Carlow, Wexford and Wicklow.'

'Dublin, Meath and Westmeath,' added the bespectacled garsún, warming to his task.

'Offaly, Cavan and Monaghan,' the Corkman continued, "till the entire country is completely covered by the sea.'

To give the Corkman his due he sounded so convincing that some patrons were already feeling sorry for themselves. There was an unprecedented demand for fresh drinks. The Corkman executed a delightful swallow which landed him half way down his pint. He spoke like a man who believed every word he was saying.

'What about the Aran Islands and the Blaskets and the rest?' I asked of this man who was either a prodigious liar or had very special information available to him. He did not answer immediately. He looked into his glass as though it were a crystal ball. He sloshed the stout about and looked me right in the eye.

'The backwash will bring 'em down,' he said cheerfully, 'there won't be a rock or a sandbank to be seen not to mind an island. All the birds will emigrate to England or America,' he spoke the last piece with baleful finality.

'The country lasted a long time,' said a small farmer from the Stacks Mountains.

'It made a great battle surely,' said another.

The conversation took another turn when someone suggested that Ireland would sink anyway because of the great weight of water from the unprecedented rains.

'We're after some of the wettest years in the history of Ireland,' said a gloomy man who made immediately for the door lest his pronouncement provoke physical retaliation. Time passed and relevant matters such as corn, hay and turf came up for discussion. The conversation was turning pedestrian, banal, in fact. The commonplace was being trotted out.

'How do you make out Cork is sinking?' I asked the stranger who I suspected of being a Corkman. At least he had a Cork accent and his hair was combed outwards from a central crease which ran in a straight line from his forehead to his poll. Only Corkmen retain this hairstyle so popular from the 1920s to the 1960s.

'How do I know Cork is sinking?' He repeated my question to ensure the widest possible audience.

'I'll tell you how I know,' he said, 'and I tell you too my friend that it's no mystery. Cork is sinking because of all the gas they're taking out of Kinsale. What do you think has kept Cork afloat for so long? Did you think there was life-belts on to it or what?'

No one made an answer. It was apparent to me that this particular Corkman was on his way to Ballybunion to join his wife and family who had either a lodge or a caravan rented there. He was merely amusing himself while taking a respite from the rigours of the road, popping back a base for the session of beer-drinking and singing that would take place later that night at an appointed hostelry.

He was, however, more than a mere bird of passage. An ordinary person would have taken no more than a single drink and made no more than a single statement before heading for the door and freedom. Here was a man who was prepared to take on a barful of Kerrymen at the ancient game of balderdash.

Some might think him brash. Others might think him forward. Whatever anyone might think it was apparent that he was a man committed to the art of living during all his waking hours. He reached for his drink and would have swallowed what was left had not a mild-mannered patron invited him to partake of another half whiskey. I was more than surprised. I had never seen this particular patron offer to buy a drink for anyone up until this time.

The Corkman declined on the grounds that he had to drive to Ballybunion and was dangerously near the alcoholic limit under which all travellers must remain if they are to drive with impunity. Although he declined the offer of a drink he showed his thanks by returning to the subject of the sinking of Cork. He shook his head dolefully before his next pronouncement.

'It might not happen in my time,' he said, 'and it might not happen in yours but happen it will when sufficient gas is taken out.'

'What a story you have for us,' said a surly individual who had earlier been refused a drink on the grounds that he was already drunk.

'It's not my story,' said the Corkman. 'I am merely stating the facts. Cork is sinking while we sit here arguing.'

'And can anything be done?' The question came from the patron who had offered to buy him a drink.

'There's only one thing to be done and that is to pump all the hot air out of Dáil Éireann into storage tanks and according as the gas is withdrawn from Kinsale let this air be piped underground in its stead.'

There were murmurs of approval from the majority of the patrons who must often have wondered if the superabundance of hot air in the Dáil would ever be utilised for the benefit of the Irish people.

Some readers will ask if it is strictly necessary to devote so much space to the visit of an unknown Corkman when other more relevant and more important matters might more profitably be aired. I respectfully submit that it is. He was different from the general run. He had something unusual to say for himself. If there were more like him the public houses of Ireland would be brighter and better places. God preserve us from churlishness, from lack of common civility and from thuggery and send us more men with cheerful dispositions and outrageous revelations like that vanished Corkman.

Jack Faulkner

On Sunday last as I was driving between Listowel and Athea I picked up a local man who asked me how it was that I never wrote about Jack Faulkner anymore. Jack is deceased of course but this is no excuse. I was glad of the question because it gives me the opportunity to recall some of Jack's comments on life and on the people he encountered as he was passing through.

Jack Faulkner was a gentle and humorous soul. Glin was his favourite town with Listowel and Abbeyfeale in close attendance.

'Collected proper,' Jack would say, 'Glin is worth a hundred pounds a year and two hundred saucers of flour, heaped.'

When he grew old Jack was presented with a house by the Glin community. The house was built on a site which had belonged to the Knight of Glin. Jack and the Knight were on friendly terms. I was present in Conway's Hotel one evening of a carnival when Jack was asked by a reporter from *The Kerryman* as to how he addressed the Knight whenever they met.

'Well,' said Jack, 'when I meets him by day I says good day Knight and when I meets him by night I says goodnight Knight.'

'I was only the once in jail,' Jack informed me one night in Glin.

Apparently he struck a Glin man outside these here premises where I presently write this very piece. He received a month.

'It was the best education I ever got,' Jack told me.

The day he was leaving the prison a guard called him after he had passed through the portals. It wanted but two days for Christmas.

'Did they give you any presents?' he asked Jack.

A shake of the head was the answer.

'That's terrible,' said the guard and so saying he drew back his boot and gave Jack a kick on the behind.

When Jack was in his heyday he was employed by the Sheridans on the occasion of Tralee horse fair. At seven-thirty in the morning Oul' Sheridan the famous horse-dealer handed him a token and told him to go for his breakfast to a nearby restaurant. When Jack arrived he took a seat near the door.

'In a strange place,' Jack explained, "tis safer stay near the door. If there's trouble you'll be the first to get away.'

Anyway, no sooner was he seated than a waitress approached and enquired if he wanted cornflakes.

'Are they boiled or roast?' Jack asked, thinking she had said corncrakes.

'Don't be funny,' said the waitress.

Jack had never heard of cornflakes and neither had a large percentage of the Irish people at that particular time.

'What's funny about it?' Jack asked but the waitress rounded on him with a verbal broadside. 'Get out of here you rotten horse-blocker,' she screamed.

Jack departed without his breakfast.

He was a true knight of the road and if there was one place he hated more than any other it was a hospital.

'It's the gas,' Jack would say, 'I can't bear it and I don't eat proper till I'm on the outside. Jail is fine but

24

don't give me hospitals.'

I remember I once met him in the city of Limerick after he had spent a time in one of the local recuperative centres. He was standing outside Cruise's Hotel looking for a lift home.

''Twas God sent you,' he said.

I invited him to have a drink but oddly enough he refused and told me that he had a fierce craving for food.

'I couldn't eat,' he explained, 'with them gas fumes flying around.'

'Look,' I said, 'come on in here to Cruise's and I'll stand you dinner before we go home.'

'Dinner!' he exclaimed with disbelief, 'and who would you get to put down spuds for you this hour of night.'

Weird but Normal

The theme of normality is a tricky one and is best left to experts or to those like myself who would chance their arm at anything provided there was some sort of assurance that I would be read and also paid for what I wrote.

The trouble is that people who elaborate on normality may not be all that normal themselves. Once we accept this we are free to expand on the theme. We must also ask ourselves did we come from normal backgrounds and if our parents or grandparents were normal. I'm not sure about mine. I know for a fact that the majority of my family were not normal. They would not be related to me otherwise.

What is a normal person? A normal person is, of course, a person skilled in the subterfuges of concealing his or her abnormalities. I had a cousin who used to remove the meat from sausage rolls on the grounds that he didn't like sausages but he did like the flavour the sausages gave the pastry. They took him to a doctor who hated the sight of sausage rolls and who informed his parents that the man was perfectly normal.

At this stage I must ask myself the question am I normal? I have often asked myself the same question privately but I do so now for the first time publicly. The answer is that I do not know for sure. Sometimes I behave normally and sometimes I behave abnormally and my real trouble is that I don't know the difference.

Here is a peculiar tale about degrees of normality

in the human or rather in a particular human. It all happened during a recent Listowel Race meeting. It was the middle night of the week-long festival. The bar was crowded and all was well, that is until a young gentleman appeared upon the scene. We were informed that he had just been released from a mental institution into the care of his brother and two friends. He was fine at the outset but then he began to act up.

He had been consigned to the institution originally because he believed he was Buffalo Bill which was all very fine until he nearly killed a man one day who told him that he didn't look in the least like Buffalo Bill.

Anyway he began to sing and dance and rant and rave so that customers began to leave the bar in fear of their lives. One even locked himself into the toilet and would not come out, not even at closing time when the bar was empty.

I was reluctantly obliged to make a complaint to the poor fellow's handlers especially when he assaulted a harmless fellow at the next table who had been sitting peacefully with his wife and sister-in-law minding his own business. All would have been well but for the sister-in-law who was an aggressive type to begin with. She flung an outsize ashtray at him but luckily she missed narrowly. She left in a huff.

'Look,' said the brother of the demented man in a most reassuring tone, 'don't take any notice of him because you can take it from me that he'll be perfect when he gets back to normal.'

Then realising that he might not have made himself clearly understood he explained for my benefit that the poor fellow would be perfectly normal as soon as he got back to believing that he was Buffalo Bill again.

Sure enough when we ignored him for a while he

calmed down and was his own self, that is to say, Buffalo Bill.

Evasion

There isn't a man or woman reading this that isn't a genius at evasion. It is part of the human make-up and it is the one thing at which we all excel. If you are not able to evade others on a regular basis, life will not be worth living. Your privacy which is one of your outstanding assets could well be irrevocably shattered by too many unwelcome intrusions. Guard your privacy as though it were your purse. In the long run it is just as valuable. I mean what's the point in having assets if you have no privacy.

The preservation of one's privacy does not call for rudeness. Neither need you be peremptory. You need not lose friends and you need not make enemies. Evasive action which is one of your chief natural resources will always do the needful. I don't mean that slipping into a side street or a shop door is the be-all and end-all of evasion. There are other methods as you shall see. If you cherish your privacy you would do well to read on.

I didn't realise until a few weeks ago how true were the words of the old refrain:

> *There's no man with endurance*
> *Like the man who sells insurance.*

There I was cautiously making my way down Grafton Street after a stroll through St Stephen's Green when suddenly I heard my name being called. Naturally I looked around.

'J.B., J.B., my oul' son,' the voice was saying. I waited and was pounced upon by a well-built middle-aged man, impeccably dressed who wrung both my hands as though I were his long-lost brother.

'Don't you remember,' he said with a loud, tooth-filled laugh, 'the Ormond. It must be twenty years ago, the night before the 1971 All-Ireland.'

I just couldn't remember so I pretended I did rather than hurt his feelings. He was such a jovial fellow that it would have been a shame to dampen his spirits.

'A drink?' he suggested. I declined.

'A coffee?' I declined just as gracefully and when he insisted I truthfully told him that I was meeting my wife at our hotel at five-thirty and that it was almost that time now.

'That's all right,' he announced cheerfully, 'I'll come along.'

I explained that my wife and I were meeting for the express purpose of having a quick bite to eat before joining up with some friends from Cahersiveen for a visit to the theatre. He persisted, told me the name of his insurance company and his rank therein. He was a pleasant soul but I had promises to keep and that was that. I could not very well tell him to vamooze. He was too decent a man.

I then performed an act which I had never tried before. I was driven to it. At the time there seemed to be no other option. I sat on my behind with my back to the shopfront. Nobody seemed to be taking any notice, well nearly nobody. There were some buskers doing likewise so I wasn't out on a limb. Then a man came along and asked if I was all right. I assured him that I was.

Meanwhile the insurance man found himself on the horns of a dilemma. Here was something outside his experience. He just did not know whether to come or go. He looked around to see if I was attracting too much undue attention and then he did it. He sat down beside me and asked me in genuine tones of concern if I was okay. I thanked him for his interest but then because time was passing I made another move I had never made before. I suddenly shook his hand, rose to my feet and like a flash I was gone, around a corner and into my hotel.

It's a true story and what makes it a memorable story is that two people in a crowded street expressed their concern about my welfare and seemed to be anxious to do something about it. Their concern stood out like the white spume of a wave in a dark and stormy ocean, nay, like a white tooth in a mouthful of black ones.

Egg-in-the-Mug

When I was a boy, beyond the misty space of twice a thousand years, as the poet tells us, there was a nickname for almost everyone. High-up people were nicknamed behind their backs while low-down people were called nicknames to their faces. It didn't matter very much to the high-up and low-down, or so it seemed, but it was different for those in-between.

They could be very sensitive about nicknames and I remember one by the name of Noggins Dee who did not like to be called Noggins at all. In fact if you called him Noggins there would be an eruption of curse words capable of permanently blistering all within earshot and if by chance Noggins had consumed the contents of a few noggins, the first person to call him Noggins would be taking his life in his hands.

He was called Noggins because he was never without a noggin of quality whiskey. A noggin, as every toper knows, is a flat, two glass bottle of whiskey. It's easily transported, easily disposed of and is as good as a flask unless, of course, you fall and break it.

Noggins is now gone to that dear clime where glasses are never empty, where there are no nicknames and as the poet says:

Where falls not hail, or rain, or any snow
Nor ever wind blows loudly.

The American Indians were masters of the nickname and nobody minded. One in particular stays in mind. Joey Brown that incomparable comedian was captured by Indians in an early comic western. As everybody knows Joey was blessed with an extraordinary large mouth. It was the dominating feature of a most engaging and well-disposed physiognomy and in the territories of the white man he was frequently called Bigmouth by ignoramuses and detractors.

The red man was far more extravagant. In his third day of capture Joey saved the life of the son of the Big Chief, a young buck by the name of Some Turkey. When word reached the Big Chief he insisted that Joey be brought before him. He slapped Joey on the back and that worthy opened his mouth and smiled. The Chief was truly impressed when he beheld the size of Joey's mouth.

'This man my brother,' said the Chief.

All the onlooking braves chanted approval. The medicine men danced and rolled their eyes heavenwards.

'What we call him?' they asked.

'We call him Big Chief Cave-in-the-Face,' said the Chief.

Everybody was delighted and they all lived happily ever after.

Shortly after that I became an Indian. So did some of my friends. Others became cowboys. One summer's day while we were bathing near a falls to the east of the town one of the cowboys went out of his depth and disappeared from view. Fortunately in the ranks of the Indians was a tall brave. Although he was only eleven he was nearly six feet. He waded out and lifted the cowboy by the hair of the head from the deep water.

'This man Big Chief,' said the rescued boy as he

33

whooped and danced around his saviour.

'What we call him?' I asked.

We were all non-plussed until one of the younger garsúns who happened to be the Big Chief's small brother came up with the answer. Of course he was possessed of inside knowledge. He knew that the Big Chief's favourite repast was a boiled egg or two but not in the orthodox fashion. He liked them mashed with butter and served in a mug.

'We call him Big Chief Egg-in-the-Mug,' said the younger brother.

Everybody was pleased except for Big Chief who went berserk. He suggested Big Chief-Who-Save-Boy-From-Water but he got no hearing.

He's in America now somewhere, the land of the Red Indians whose style of nickname we had borrowed. In a few short years his deed was forgotten but the name remained.

To us he will always be Big Chief Egg-in-the-Mug.

English Words ... but the Accent is Irish

'**G**'out you waggabone!' The order was directed to a drunken wrenboy who came without flute, banjo or bodhrán and who smelled so strongly of stale porter that he could well be described as a walking brewery.

A lesser man might have termed him a drunken wretch or an alcoholic hoor but I feel that a waggabone was fairest under the circumstances. That time, which was fifty years ago of a snowy St Stephen's Day in the Stacks Mountains, the letter V was rarely used by country folk. Hence the expression 'g'out you waggabone!' which was simply a minor corruption of 'Get out you vagabond!'

The people of that time and clime would hardly know what a vagabond was but everybody knew that a waggabone was a harmless, useless fellow always on the make.

When the waggabone was told to get out he sidled sheepishly and drunkenly up to the fire and awaited the bottle of stout which he knew to be his right as soon as the civilities were disposed of. When he was asked after a while if he would care for a bottle of stout he simply answered, 'very well'.

It is still the same in the Stacks Mountains, all through Renagown, Glounamucmae and Tubbernanoon as well as Dromadomore and Knockadirreen. The Irish accent remains and you cannot but fail to hear it should you care to sojourn in Carrigcannon or Knock-nagoshel. It's alive and well and beautiful, this language with the English words and the Irish accent. It's as though the accent was waiting for the Irish language to return.

Another time; it could have been 1933 or 1934 or 1935. Anyway it was at the height of the exotic lunacy known as the Economic War which lasted from 1932 to 1938 and which almost totally impoverished the unfortunate Irish farmer who had geared himself to beef production with a view to entering the British Market. I won't go into the ins and outs of the 'War' but it was declared by De Valera who argued that no money should be paid to British landlords for land which they had stolen in the first place.

Dev had a point but the British imposed huge tariffs on Irish imports and vice versa so that the upshot of the entire ruction was that Ireland found itself with a surplus of calves. They had to be disposed of and soon, according to opposition members of Dáil Éireann, their corpses were blocking the eyes of bridges in the villages and townlands of rural Ireland but what has all this to do with our story the rapidly tiring reader will be sure to ask. I'm coming to it. In Lyreacrompane proper I was a guest one day at dinner in the home of a highly unsuccessful small farmer who happened to be a distant relation of my late, lamented father.

There was, steaming on a large dish in the centre of the table, a hind quarter of roast veal. Now roast veal is not the real thing unless it is well basted with bacon lard during its cooking. Also the proper gravy to accompany this delightful dish is best made when chopped onions are added to the fat after the veal has been removed from the roasting pot. Add some water and some thickening and allow the chopped onions to simmer.

There may be tastier dishes in the world but if there are I have neither heard of them nor tasted them. Anyway just as we were about to dive in the 'boy' as he was called stood up and announced that he would not be partaking of the fare in front of him.

'Pray why not?' his employer asked with great annoyance.

'Because,' said the boy, 'wale makes me womit!'

It was a curt retort, curt as you will find in the long litany of excuses which have been tended by farmers' boys down through the ages when they found themselves unwilling to indulge in the ordinary fare of the kitchen table.

Translated into townie language what he was saying was: 'Veal makes me vomit', which was a fabrication to put it mildly for there was a totally inexplicable aversion to roast veal in rural Ireland throughout the Economic War and for several years afterwards.

'Well,' said the farmer, 'wale don't make me womit.' Then he addressed himself to me: 'Do it make you?' he asked.

Entering into the spirit of the thing I answered, 'No, wale don't make me womit nayther.'

'Shut up you wiper,' said the farmer's boy, 'or I'll wulcanise you.'

As things turned out he did not vulcanise me for like all braggarts who make outrageous threats he was quite incapable of carrying one out. Later in the afternoon when the hunger caught him he consumed the wale and it did not make him womit! He also ate the wegetables and in no time at all he made large quantities of both wale and wegetables to wanish.

Once in Dirha bog while partaking of lunch with some other bog-workers one came out with the observation: 'These wittles is wile.'

Nobody agreed with him for like many a man at the time he did not like fat. He would eat nothing but lean whereas the reasonable man would eat both fat and lean and do himself more good than harm.

The man who intimated that the wittles were wile made objection in the first place because there were no buns on offer after the main repast had been consumed. Neither was there a small pot of black or red jam which was often included with the general fare.

He refused to eat but later in the day he announced to another bogman that his stomach was beginning to wibrate. There is only one known cure for wibrations of the stomach and that is to fill the stomach in question with food. Alas and alack, however, all the food had been consumed so the wibrations intensified until at last relief arrived in the shape of a thunderous belch which his fellow bogmen believed had uprooted all the evil gases which had lurked in the depths of this man's interior for years and years.They said this to console him and to make atonement for their having eaten his share of the rations and for having enjoyed them no end.

'Werily,' said one who had spent several weeks studying for the priesthood before being kicked out on his ear for totally depleting a year's stock of altar wine, 'you'll be wisited by peace and werily your stomach will be wiolent no more and your woice will be the woice of the lark!'

So when you hear a man, dear reader, who submerges the V and emerges with a W remember that you are not listening to a rustic who is not distorting words or letters. Rather are you listening to a man who is being absolutely faithful to his Gaelic heritage and who has said to himself in turmoil and anguish: 'To V or not to V. That is the question', and who, at the end of the day, decided not to V but to W!

The Name of Money

Men who leave fortunes behind them are rarely remembered for long. When the resources they so carefully husbanded through life are exhausted by the profligate heirs so does the memory of the benefactor also expire. I'm not saying we should not leave our possessions to our heirs. What I am saying is that we should not leave too much behind us. We should endeavour to measure out our possessions with care so that we derive the maximum benefit over our closing days in particular.

If you want to be remembered by your relations the best thing to do is leave a few modest debts behind you. You won't be remembered affectionately but you will be remembered. In fact every time a payment is made to reduce the debt you left behind, your name will be drawn down by whoever it was that was saddled with it.

In the street where I was born there was an old man who spent his declining years in the houses of several different relations. He had a crumbling, thatched house of his own in the suburbs but it was not fit for human habitation. He was therefore invited to stay with one of his relations. He was not invited out of the goodness of their hearts. He had the name of money and having the name of money is just as important as having money.

He once owned a farm but what the relations did not know was that he invested the price in liquid assets. A legacy left to him by an aunt also went down his gullet. So addicted to drink was the poor fellow that he once sold a pair of pyjamas to cure a hangover and slept in his shirt for the remainder of his life. In fact I knew a man who sold his false teeth so that he might satisfy his craving for porter. On a personal basis I was caught on a few occasions to secure people for bicycles, beds and radios. As soon as I signed on the dotted line they promptly sold the articles for which I had secured them and left me holding the baby. They sold them for drink. My problem was that I found it difficult to say no to people apart altogether from the fact that those I secured would have been far-out relations of mine.

My problem was unexpectedly solved one morning as I sat at breakfast with some total strangers in a south Kerry farmhouse whose proprietors had contracted to supply us with bed and breakfast. Sitting opposite me was a tall, lean, pious-looking man of advanced years. One word borrowed another and the subject of securing people came up. I think I may have casually said that I could afford several holidays if those I secured had honoured their commitments.

The pious-looking man said in the most offhand of manners, 'I was asked recently by a cousin to secure him for a motor cycle. I just told him that civil servants could not secure, that they would be dismissed the moment it came to the attention of their employers.' The ploy worked. I then explained that I was not a civil servant.

'Have you a brother or sister who is a civil servant?' he asked. I told him that I had a brother who was.

'Tell those who want you to secure them,' said he, 'that your brother will be sacked without redress if you secure anybody.'

41

It worked. The next time I was asked I explained to the female who wished to exploit me, and not for the first time either, that my brother's job would be at risk if I obliged her. 'He's a civil servant,' I informed her emphatically, 'and you know what happens when a family member secures someone.'

Rather than admit ignorance she nodded her head solemnly.

But where is all this leading us and what about the man who came to live with his relations? He lived first with one and then with the others. He would spend a maximum of about three months with each. He made notes of their particular kindnesses in a jotter especially bought for the purpose. He would enter sums of money borrowed and the cost of special foodstuffs like lamb's liver and sausage rolls. All would be revealed in his will and all who maintained him would be well rewarded.

When he died he left not a single penny behind him but he left several relations who would never forget him. They had invested heavily in him and there was one in particular who plied him with expensive cakes after his dinner. She saw him in much the same light as the post office, a good solid investment which would be there for the taking the moment he permanently closed his peepers.

The bother with investing in humans who have the name of money is that there is a high risk factor. You cannot really believe humans when it comes to money so that I would be tempted to advise the investor to stick with the post office or a reliable building society or even the banks. At least your money will be safe whereas with the relation who has the name of money there is no guarantee whatsoever and remember too that he will be safely out of reach when the will is read and it is discovered that he has nothing.

Different if the person you invest with has a conscience. He will leave sufficient to meet the requirements of the investors. Alas the party without a conscience will lead the investor all the way to the grave with false promises and nothing to back them up. I have seen cases where bankrupt investors were even saddled with the cost of the funeral. I have even seen investors supply an abundance of drink and food on the strength of a will which had not yet been read.

By all means help out a worse off relative. Even go so far as to buy him delicacies but do not expect anything in return. You should try to remember that virtue is its own reward and that charity begins at home. 'Whatsoever you do in my name,' saith the Lord, 'it shall be rewarded one hundredfold in heaven.' Alas there are too many who just will not wait for heaven. They want their heaven right here on earth and they want it by way of large fortunes left by relatives. It's all a matter of attitudes. I remember once to hear it said of a friend of my father's that he drank out two farms. The woman who disclosed the poor man's folly shook her head sadly as she spoke whereas an old man who disclosed the same story in a pub around the same time, shook his head in admiration. I'm all for leaving something behind. Don't get me wrong on that score. What I have will go with a good heart to my next of kin. However to leave them too much would be bad for them and there is the danger that I would be obliged to neglect myself were I to aim too high on their behalf.

Enough is enough and anything more is merely a surfeit. I would not perform as Tom Daly did. I would not do away with it all before I died. Still his will was a chastening one and should be a reminder to expectant relatives. 'Being of sound mind,' Tom wrote, 'I drank every halfpenny I had before I died'.

Extra-Judicial

I was standing one evening by the Black Rocks in Ballybunion when a man approached me out of the sandhills. Darkness was imminent and the sea birds had withdrawn gracefully from the sky. In the distance across the sea a light-house blinked and the outline of an outbound tanker stood sharply against the horizon.

It was, as you have surmised, a seaside scene. I might, if I so wished, make reference to other maritime matters but we are not here to paint a picture. There is a story to be told so that the picture will have to wait for another time.

The man from the sandhills was impeccably dress-ed, new brown sandals, white socks, white shirt open at the neck, white handkerchief in the lapel of light grey sports-coat and a good quality grey flannel pants. He looked respectable as well, with his rimless spectac-les and his gold tooth high-lighting the snowy white-ness of its natural companions. There was only one thing amiss. His hair, albeit scant and somewhat grey, was tousled. It was totally out of character for he was not the type of man atop whose head you would expect to see tousled hair.

'Wind's from a good quarter,' he observed in a re-fined and cultured tone.

'So it is,' I answered agreeably although I had paid no particular attention to the wind's vagaries up to the time of his revelation.

'Be dark soon,' he said and waited for me to ac-

45

company him back to civilisation. I went along and we matched paces. He struck me as the kind of man to whom an uneven step would be total anathema and yet he wasn't an army man. I suspected he had spent some time in the local defence forces. In those days they had the name of producing more martinets than ordinary soldiers. I didn't tell you when all these events took place. It was about 1948 or 1949, at the latest.

It also struck me as we were walking along, militarily more or less, that he was not the type of chap one would expect to see emerging from the sandhills with tousled hair at approximately ten o'clock in the evening. From time to time he would look around him furtively and I sensed that he was using me. His business in the sandhills while certainly his own may not have been strictly above board and I suspected from the tousled hair which he had just started to comb, that he was returning from an illicit tryst with some female who must surely have availed of an alternative exit. As we climbed the concrete steps from the strand he paused and with a spotless white hand indicated the beauty of the vista to our rear. The sun was sinking and a roseate glow turned the sea at the distant horizon to burnished gold. Then the sun sank and we resumed our journey, mine to the Pavilion Ballroom where I had a date which might and might not materialise and he to heaven-knows-where and heaven-knows-what. As we walked past the Castle Hotel he took his leave and I never saw him again.

Just then I ran into a member of the garda síochána who chanced to be off duty. We walked up the street together and turned into Mikey Joe's American Bar for a drink. Mikey was only a garsún then but in appearance he still retains his garsúnhood and it looks now that he will never grow old. Inside we availed ourselves of the snug which was empty of patrons at the time. Two pints of stout were called for and as they were being dispensed my friend spoke for the first time.

'I saw you talking to Rodney,' he said.

'Was that his name?' I asked.

'Yes,' said my friend, 'Rodney Gillespie.'

I am not proffering his real name for the good reason that he may still be alive or, worse still, the woman he met that very evening might still be with us and if she were it would be folly as well as mischief to mention her name. We shall therefore call her Gladioli for the good reason that I have never in my life met a woman called Gladioli. Anyway to proceed with our story I informed my companion how Rodney had more or less strung me along until we reached the Castle Hotel.

'The wife would be staying there,' my friend told me, 'and you'd be a nice cover for him on his way from the meeting with Gladioli. Would you believe,' this most informative member of the force confided, 'that he's every day of sixty-six and she's a year older and yet they meet year in, year out every July down the sandhills just as the sun is declining.'

He forestalled my next question by lifting his pint, by surveying it at length in a fashion which brooked no further interference and by quaffing about one-third of it in a single appreciative swallow. He wiped the froth from his moustache and settled himself before proceeding.

'They are both married,' he explained, 'but not to each other and this is always a problem.' He reached

47

for his pint a second time and took a goodly swallow before calling for the same again.

'I have to go back on duty at ten-thirty,' he said.

For a while there was silence as becomes a snug and then, because he knew that I was possessed of a curious nature, he proceeded with his narrative.

'Apparently,' he explained, 'Rodney and Gladioli were once sweethearts but Fate intervened and he was forced into exile. He went to America and she promised to follow. Alas he fell among deceivers in the Land of the Free and was blinded by the city lights. For a while he forgot poor Gladioli who pined for him all the while in Erin's green isle. He accumulated money and married into society. Time passed and when his family was reared he and his American spouse found themselves holidaying in Ballybunion. One evening as he was wandering absently through the sandhills who should he see in the distance, and she ambling too, but Gladioli. In a thrice they were in each other's arms. Alas she had married too. They found they were still in love and promised to meet, without fail, each year in the same place at the same hour which was approximately sunset.

'Did they become lovers?' I asked.

'I am not a peeping Tom so I can't tell you that,' he replied. 'However,' he continued, 'I will tell you this and it is that if I were asked to recommend a prime location for an extra-judicial trysting-place I would have no hesitation in nominating the Ballybunion sandhills.'

My date at the Pavilion materialised and fortunately she's still with me. As for my friend who told me the story; well he has departed the scene God bless him. I still remember his smiling face, his gentlemanly manner and his perfectly-trimmed white moustache. Ballybunion hasn't been the same since he passed away.

Play the Fool

'If fools were scarce he'd make two'. Don't ask me where I heard that statement. It could have been anywhere, radio, television or the pub. It could have been the street. It matters not, however, where it was heard. What really matters is that I remember it and present it here for your titillation.

It recalls for me too how facilely we dismiss people with the disdainful observation that they are fools. 'Don't mind him,' we say, 'he's nothing but a fool'. But is he a fool? He may talk like a fool and be regarded as a fool by those who would be better advised to retain their sentiments but for all this he knows how to make out in the world. I'll give you an instance.

Years ago we were all seated at the dinner table in my father's house. There was a good dinner in front of us. Midway through the meal a young man entered. He was from another part of town but he used to run with us as children and consequently a place was made for him at the table. He had just returned from England where he had left his job and come home for a holiday. He dined well. In fact, as my father was later to recall, he polished off twice as much as any of us. He regaled us with tales of his life abroad in a slightly affected accent. When he finished eating he accepted a cigarette and when the cigarette was alight he took his leave.

When he was gone he came in for some severe criticism. Listowel then as now was no different from any other small town in its capacity for character ass-

assination. We referred to his accent and we referred to his tall tales and we referred to the payslips which he had shown us. It was the fashion of the time for young chaps working in England to bring home their payslips, especially overtime ones, in order to show how well they were doing across the sea.

We had several good laughs at his expense but then my father made one of his rare observations. He was a man seldom given to commentary and when he spoke it nearly always made sense. 'You think he's a fool!' he opened as he cleaned out the bowl of his pipe with a penknife. We did not answer. We were not meant to. He looked at each face in turn, pursed his lips and returned to the evisceration of the pipe bowl. 'I say he's a very clever fellow indeed,' my father went on, 'far cleverer fellow than any of you.'

At this stage we felt we were entitled to a laugh and laugh we did although it was a rather hollow one for we suspected that he was setting us up as he frequently did. Like a skilled boxer he would allow us to indulge in our little vagaries for awhile and then flatten us with a series of clever punches.

'He's no more a fool,' he went on, 'than I am. In fact if I was pressed in a court of law I would say that I was a bigger fool than he is.'

More laughter. Then my younger sister intervened. 'But,' said she, 'you're a schoolmaster.'

We all laughed, my father the loudest of all.

'Let us recap,' he said. We listened attentively although all of the males of the household, myself excluded because of my youth, had indulged in a few pre-prandial drinks earlier in Alla Sheehy's pub next door. 'Firstly,' my father had opened, 'he's no fool because of his timing. He knew when we would be having our dinner so he called at that time knowing full well that he would be provided with an excellent meal free of charge. Secondly he got himself a free cigarette in spite of the fact that they are severely rationed and thirdly he promised that he would call again which means that he is a very smart chap indeed because the chances are that he will call again during a meal and so provide himself with free fare for a second and maybe a third and fourth time before he decides to go back to England.'

We sat chastened while my father filled his pipe with the cut plug to which he was addicted. Before applying the lighted match to the innards of the pipe bowl he spoke as follows 'I say to you,' he said solemnly, 'the man that would burn him for a fool would have wise ashes.'

My mother who had been silent up to this joined in. Now she didn't always agree with my father.

'Often,' said she, 'a fellow only seems a fool,' and she went to tell us about a neighbour of her acquaintance who played the fool to suit himself when she was a young girl in the footballing province of Ballydonoghue which lies between Listowel and Ballybunion. 'Everyone,' my mother continued, 'thought he was a fool. This was because he played the fool so well that nobody ever sent him on errands which called for responsibility and nobody asked him to help with the turf-cutting or the hay-making.'

My mother went on to explain that no local farmer would trust him with a shovel lest he do damage to himself or others. Bad as a shovel might be the prospect of what he might do with a pike did not bear thinking about so they left him alone. They even went so far as to cut his turf for him. He had no land so they did not have to make his hay.

'But he was no fool,' my mother insisted,' he was an able buck and as soon as he went to America they found out that he was far from being the fool he was painted at home. You see,' my mother went on God be good to her, 'in America it's a case of have it yourself or be without it. 'Tis us here at home that were real fools. We fed and we looked after him and when we had him reared he left us without as much as a thank you. He was able to use a pike and well able to use a shovel but work didn't agree with him.'

To further buttress the fact he was no fool he married well. She was a lady twenty years older and when she eventually worked herself into the grave on his behalf he came back to Ireland and married again, this time a schoolteacher.

'And to think,' said my mother, 'that we thought him a fool. 'Tis now I know who the fools were.'

So there's a messy moral. Play the fool to be thought a fool and you'll even get away with murder!

The Nine Rules for Corner Boys

Over the years I have been invited by as many as twenty readers to visit some of the corners in their native towns and villages to view the many fine specimens of corner boys on view there. I have always declined for I believe that while it is all right to write about one's own corner boys it is improper to intrude upon the domains of others.

If, for instance I were to spend, say six months or a year, in the vicinity of an authenticated corner boy pitch then I might very well sit down and turn out a thousand words on the denizen or denizens therein but even then I would not be happy that I had produced no more than superficial conclusions. No. It is best to concentrate on one's very own corner. One is then aware of the terrain and one may relate the arrival of a new corner boy to his surroundings without too much difficulty.

The letters I receive begin something like this; 'you must come and see our corner boy'. This opening would be followed by a colourful description of the corner boy in question. They believe that by spending an afternoon looking at and speaking to a candidate for the position of corner boy that all will be revealed so to speak. The truth is that I would require several months of the most acute observation under a massive set of varying circumstances to deduce whether or not the boy at any given corner was really a corner boy.

Corner girls do not exist. If they did I would be the first to write about them. For obvious reasons girls may not stand at corners all day long. Prurient and ignorant minds have seen to that. The corner therefore, is the exclusive property of boys. For boys you may take men.

To tell the truth I find it difficult to pass through a strange town without inspecting the corner boys on view. I would find myself quite accidentally in the same vicinity of the corner in a distant town and would recall that the very same corner had been recommended to me by a reader.

Without seeming to do so I would observe the resident corner boy and after a while might even ask him the location of the post office. If he chanced to be a communicative corner boy I might very well draw down the state of the weather and if he were a very well-disposed corner boy I might even share his corner for a while. Sometimes I would just sidle up to the corner as if I had been acquainted with it for years and pretend to draw a sigh of relief at having met up with it once more.

Then there are readers who write and ask if it's really true that I can tell a corner boy at a glance. The answer is no. My advice to those who wish to know whether their corners are playing host to bogus or genuine corner boys is to look to the following guidelines:–

First make sure that your corner is a regulation corner i.e. a substantial street on either side.

Secondly make sure your corner boy is fully clothed i.e. shortcoat, trousers, shirt, shoes, etcetera. A true corner boy will never be seen at a corner without his shortcoat, not even in sweltering heat.

Thirdly if your corner boy is drunk he is bogus. A real corner boy uses his corner as an observation post and not a support for drunkenness.

Fourthly a true corner boy will never queer his own pitch i.e. crush his cigarette butt, puke, piddle or whatever at any hour of the day or night. Neither will he spit or finger-blow his nose. He will remove himself to another area for all the foregoing purposes.

Fifthly he never stands with his hands into his trousers pockets. He always keeps his hands behind his back.

Sixthly he never calls a visitor to the corner by his name although the identity of the caller may be well known to him. This is to discourage permanency of residence.

The corner boy is a past member of the withering look. He knows that his claim to sole proprietorship of any corner will not stand up in court. He must therefore resort to other non-violent means in order to preserve his claim. The withering look will discourage all pretenders if it is properly brought to bear. I have seen outsize, accredited thugs wilt before it. The dog may be the master of the nerve-shattering bark and the lion the paralyser of his prey with his mighty roar but when it comes to withering looks we have to hand it to the corner boy.

Seventh your fully-qualified corner boy will not be influenced by weather. Hail, rain or shine he will stick to his difficult task by the simple expedient of removing himself to the other side of the corner when one side is besieged by the elements. But what if the rain is not driven by the wind? What if it falls straight down from the skies overhead? What then? The corner boy will simply pull his shortcoat up over his head and conceal himself as best he can in the corner door-way. Every corner has at least one doorway a few steps away from where the corner boy normally stands

Eighth and this is most important. If he is the genuine article he will always touch his forelock in the presence of a member of the garda síochána. Whatever else he might be, the genuine corner boy is no fool. He knows that the garda is the only authority with the power to remove him. All the guard has to say is 'move along there!' and the jig is up.

We all know the corner boy is no loiterer but you try proving that in court and you're in for a big suck-in. We all know that he is no obstructionist but proving it on a busy day with hundreds of people passing could well be beyond the scope of the most skilful advocate.

Ninth and finally your true corner boy is like a Greek chorus. He watches life go on around him but never permits himself to become involved. That is why he is always so reluctant to answer questions. It is not that he is churlish. It is that he does not wish to fall out of character. But what is the role of the corner boy? It is to be there, to witness, to play his part, however fragile, in the ongoing turmoil without complaint or observation. When he stands at a corner he is marking himself present and on Judgment Day will be able to say – 'I held my corner. I could do no more'.

Plateau Erosion

'I find most men's hair grimy and sorely in want of washing. Give me a bald man any day'.

The foregoing was overheard by me on my way from Ballybunion by bus several years ago. The reason I chanced to be travelling by bus was because I had over-imbibed. It was the afternoon of the 15 August which is the Pattern Day in Ballybunion. I left my car outside Mikey Joe O'Connor's Irish-American Bar and availed myself of public transport. My missus and myself would collect our car later that night after I had dined and snoozed. I would have been home earlier but I met some relations from the Cashen.

'Give me a bald man any day'. The saying still lingers with me. From time to time I have listened to and been involved in arguments concerning the merits of the hairy and the bald.

The other night, in fact, in the bar, a woman chanced to be speaking about her second husband. She had, if you will forgive the expression, been around the matrimonial course three times in all. The much-lamented trio are now subscribing to the upkeep of numerous, proverbial daisies in the same plot happily resting without a word or a wink between them.

'Of the three,' said she, 'the bald man was the best and 'tis me that knows for I spent ten years with each of 'em.'

According to this much-bereaved widow the bald-headed man was the strongest of the three, the most ardent and ferocious lover, the cleanest by far from a physical point of view and add to all this the fact that he could have any female he clapped his eye on.

'Except,' said his widow proudly, 'that I was plenty for him.'

At the time she happened to be drinking with a friend of indeterminate age. In short she might have been anything from forty-five to seventy. Said she quietly and without raising as much as an eyelid, 'the only one you'll hear taking away from a bald-headed man is a man what isn't. It don't make no difference to a woman. It's the man what matters and not the hair on his head.'

Come to think about it. You'd never hear a female calling a man baldy. Only garsúns and older men do that. The way the male of the species speak about bald-ness in others you'd think it was a crime to have no hair on one's head. A woman truly knows the value of a man and none knows better that a curly-headed buck could often break your heart whereas a bald-headed man would painstakingly put it together again. I am not writing in defence of baldness. I don't have to. Bald men have proved themselves before I was born and before my grandfather and his grandfather were born. The prejudice against bald men has existed just as long. It is, I believe, a prejudice born out of jealousy. I rem-ember in Ballybunion when I was in my heyday, tripp-ing the light fantastic in the Pavilion Ballroom to the dulcet strains of Pat Crowley's inimitable orchestra, never to have seen a bald man who couldn't dance cheek-to-cheek to the delight of his partner.

At the time it was a brave man who publicly danced cheek-to-cheek. If one was to believe visiting missioners it was a transgression which deserved excommunication. I remember too to have been at a football game in Tralee between Kerry and Clare or it may well have been Tipperary. Contrary to all expectations Kerry took a drubbing at midfield and all at the hands of a powerfully-made, bald-headed Clareman. Repeatedly he went higher than his Kerry counterparts which was no mean feat in those days. His name escapes me but maybe there's a reader who recalls him. Anyway there he was, unbeatable in the centre, when a profane lout shouted out 'Go 'long you baldy hoor'. The action that prompted the verbal onslaught was precipitated by the bald man. He met a dour opponent shoulder to shoulder and he was still on his feet when the clash was over. He seized a high ball immediately and, as though to prove to the foul-mouthed onlooker that a bald man was as good as any, he sent the ball between the posts from fifty yards range for the equalising point.

On a personal note I am a man who has been afflicted by plateau erosion for some years now. This simply means that I am losing my hair which is as it should be. However I must say that it has improved my performances in all my commitments rather than detracting from them. I have not yet lost all my hair and maybe I never will. What matters is that I will cherish baldness should it come. I will endeavour to be a worthy host to a bald head and I hope to live up to the high standards set by other men with hairless nappers.

When I laboured for my crust in England I got to know a young Welsh doctor who could not wait to be bald. He was handicapped in his search for mature professionalism by a cherubic face which took from rather than added the much-desired age to his unblemished countenance. His family had all been beset by early baldness but when I bade him farewell he had nothing to show by way of reduction in his wavy fleeces. What is it then that makes one man want to keep baldness at bay and another anxious to be overcome by it? It all boils down to vanity, to not being content with our lots. We seem never to know when we are all well off. How's that Pope puts it:

> *Hope springs eternal in the human breast;*
> *Man never Is, but always To be blest.*

I would be more than happy if I were to experience all the stages of plateau erosion from the first falling rib to the last. How noble it is to turn from black to grey as the years go by and to fulfil oneself naturally as time whitens the plateau. After grey come the silvery tints which are occasioned by a dominance of white over grey and then comes the white when the human plateau is crowned with snow. Then comes the melting of the snow and the dear old plateau is left bare and isn't this wonderful too! We see the seasons reflected on our changing and eventually disappearing ribs.

To those who seek to be covered with waves or curls or hanging locks I say unto you; are not the mountaintops bald and I ask you if there is a solitary rib of hair to be seen on the crimson horizon as the sun seeks its rest. Better be bright and bald than grimy and unkempt. Remember too that he travels fastest who travels alone. By this I mean that a heavy mohal of hair is no ally when one is fleeing from his enemies.

The Music of Humanity

Many years ago while in the village of Carraigkerry during a carnival I found myself in a public house in the middle of a huge crowd of people. I believe I have referred briefly to this incident before but a letter from a reader in Leeds requests me to recall that marvellous occasion for her. She comes from the district in question and was a young girl when the incident occurred.

It was Sunday night in the height of summer as I set out from Listowel with three companions. Happily all are in the land of the living save one. The deceased is Dan Kennelly, the well-known Listowel publican. The living are Jerome Murphy, the popular Listowel auctioneer originally from Glashnagook, Knockna-goshel and the other is Jimmy Boylan, a retired uphol-sterer from the city of Cork.

It was Jimmy Boylan who came to my aid when I strove to resurrect the occasion. He has a prodigious memory and as luck would have it he happens to be holidaying in these premises right now.

'I often think of that night,' he said, 'and the magic that was in it.'

Anyway to proceed with the tale we departed Lis-towel at approximately seven-thirty. We stopped in the beautiful village of Athea to slake our respective thirsts and after spending an hour in extremely congenial company in two of the village's more engaging public houses we proceeded on our journey.

Carraigkerry was packed to capacity or, as the man

said, you couldn't draw your leg. However, crowded as the streets were, the public houses were crammed entirely and it was either a brave man or a genuinely thirsty one who would venture through the portals of any one. We decided, therefore, to postpone a public house visit for awhile so that we might take in the musical delights on offer.

There was no scarcity of musicians. I remember we encountered the late and great Jack Faulkner who welcomed us officially. Jack always said that his full name was Jack Wilberforce Faulkner but the trouble with Jack was that you never knew whether he was codding you or not. Otherwise he was a great soul with a profound sense of humour and his welcome put the seal on what was to be a memorable occasion.

Eventually, because of the attention we paid to the many musicians who played out of doors we found ourselves mentally exhausted. Mental exhaustion is the very thing to put an edge on the thirst so once more we found ourselves drawn to the public house. We chose the nearest one to where we found ourselves. We were warmly greeted by patrons and publican alike. Standing room was made for us and we were welcomed into that most intoxicating of brotherhoods often referred to by the abstemious as the drinking classes.

Here were no gentlemen as such nor were any landed gentry apparent. Here was the heart's blood of the Irish countryside with its own music, its own money and its own capacity to absorb strong drink in all its forms and all this, remember, without the least vestige of hostility, rancour or coarse language.

Our wants were simple. Four small Irish whiskies. Clutching our glasses to our breasts we stood in the middle of the crowd exchanging pleasantries and warmly responding to the many fine welcomes extended unstintingly by the good folk of West Limerick.

Then we heard it, faint at first but gradually growing in volume until our voices were stilled, so rapt was our admiration for the heavenly music which assailed our ears.

It was fiddle music, of course. We looked around for the musician. He stood nearby with his eyes closed, his bow moving gently across the strings and an unsurpassed melody pouring out from the soul of the venerable instrument which he clasped.

'What's that you're playing?' one of our party asked.

'I'm not playing,' he responded with a smile.

'But it's your fiddle,' we told him, 'and it's your hand that is directing the bow.'

'It is not my hand,' he explained, 'it is the hands of all men.'

He went further for our enlightenment and informed us that it was the stirrings of the throng of people which governed the movements of the bow.

'Look,' he said, as the crowd swayed, 'the people are pushing against my arm. It's their music, not mine.'

What he said was true. The bow moved over the strings, impelled by the human beings all around.

'It's the music of humanity,' said the fiddler, 'praise be to God for all things.'

Tyranny

I knew a man one time, a distant relation of mine in fact, who was possessed of one daughter and five sons. I do not use the word possessed lightly. Possess the daughter he did in the sense that he would not allow suitors to call nor did he want to hear mention of young men she met at dances or elsewhere. Often by the fire when all the family was present he would speak to himself.

'I will cut the head clear and clane off the first man to go near her,' he would open. When his words had sunk in he would start again.

'I'll tear his heart out so I will and I'll give it to the cat if he so much as lays a ludeen on her.'

The family would listen obediently. The girl, we'll call her Mary, was eighteen when the paternal fulminations began. Then the years went by and she reached the age of thirty-one without a single proposal of marriage.

'And how would anyone propose to her?' the mother would say to the girl's brothers, 'when her father has the fear of God put into every eligible bachelor in the seven parishes?'

The mother would never speak to her husband and never once did she bare her feelings towards him. You see he was a male tyrant, a man who dismissed women as chattels even when one of those very women was his wife.

He would brook contradiction in nothing. If she

65

dared venture an opinion he would shout her down. There aren't as many male tyrants as there used to be but one is one too many in a country where men got away with everything for years. I personally remember in the street where I was born there were six practising male tyrants who treated their womenfolk like dirt. In the countryside there were several others who often put their women out of the house for periods and left them to walk up and down the road in the dark of the night.

They got away with it because the women in question came from a long line of domestic slaves and it seemed that both Church and State were combining against them. They were not at liberty to have opinions and they were not at liberty to enter public houses or go to the cinemas or circuses alone for instance.

What they were at liberty to do was to have more children than was good for their health and they were at liberty as well to work from dawn till night without let-up. The wheel is turning but it would want to be spun at a breakneck speed for a long time if we are ever to make amends.

Anyway to get back to the unmarried Mary at the age of thirty-one. It looked as though she would remain on the shelf forever. In public houses her father would describe the punishment he would inflict upon those who might even look sideways at his daughter. There was one individual in particular in whose company he had once seen her outside the parish church. All the fellow did was chat up the daughter but in the father's eyes this was tantamount to first degree rape. 'If I catch him,' said the parent, 'he'll wish he was dead. Better he be borned a rat or a flea when he's done with me. Better he come into the world a bloody louse.'

When he saw the same man chatting her up a second time he went home and gave his poor wife a thump in the stomach for no reason at all.

'When I lay hands on him,' he roared, 'I'll cut off his ten toes and stick them up his behind and then I'll stitch his buttocks together with thorny wire. Better he be borned a maggot.'

The following day his daughter disappeared. She went off to England with her man and in the course of a year she sent for her mother.

The sons followed suit and it must be said that all lived happily ever after with the exception of the father. He brooded by his fire until he expired from the weight of the grime and the dirt which he accumulated for seven unwashed years. Everyone was agreed that he got his just entitlements.

I knew him personally. I was young and, therefore, constituted no threat to his daughter. All he ever did while I sat in his kitchen was give out about his wife. She went around gently and silently with a stoop to her, a saint and a martyr if there ever was one.

In England she blossomed into a habitual and outstanding bingo player. She went to the pub at weekends where she sang and danced with men of her own age who never stopped showering praise on her. She even fell in love and was loved in return.

To make up for years of neglect she had her hair done once a week instead of once a year while she was at home and she was promoted to supervisor in the factory where she had become a machine operator. All tyrants please take note.

Importance of Being Refined

I once knew a woman who was very refined and, more importantly, unlike most refined women, she was refined all the time. Many refined women are only refined some of the time.

Circumstances, I fear, refine us and unrefine us. To be refined is to be free of impurities. It is also to affect nicety and subtlety so that it should be said that refinement is acquired. We are not born with it. What we are born with is the capacity to make ourselves refined.

The woman I knew wasn't too refined. I could not bear her if she was. She was always fairly refined and they said of her that she took this refinement with her to her grave. To be too refined is an awful curse like Stevie Smith's 'Englishwoman':

> *This Englishwoman is so refined*
> *She has no bosom and no behind.*

Now there's refinement for you. Some people don't care how much they suffer if their refinement shows. While they may not wish to impose their refinement they nevertheless like to be seen being refined.

The arch-enemy of refinement is, alas, the indiscreet breaking of wind, that odious revelation of the posterus which can deflate even the most highly-bred, the most cultured, the most temperate and the least abrasive of personalities.

It can all come crashing down should this malodorous squeak escape its confines. It's all right if the breaking is silent. Others can be blamed, even the most unlikely, even royals or monsigniori or generals or admirals for no man and no woman is free from the occasional indiscretion.

One may belch at will for there is a method of countering the belch which can even enhance the belcher. This can be accomplished by pressing the forefinger and its neighbour to the lips in gentle atonement. All is forgiven at once but not so the breaking of wind. The weakness, always there, has been identified and the refined party is no longer seen as refined.

Refinement used to be aimed at as a matter of course by all young ladies in Victorian times and to a lesser degree during my own boyhood. Girls would go out of their way to flaunt their gentility but this in itself was the very antithesis of refinement for it is by not flaunting that we really show how refined we are.

'But who wants to be refined?' the unrefined will ask. Come now. You'd be surprised. There is a hunger for refinement in those who would protest the loudest.

There's no harm at all in being refined so long as it isn't over done. I would not have brought up the subject at all but for overhearing a local theatregoer who chanced to visit these premises the other night.

She had just left the theatre where she and her friends had been entertained by a play. They liked the play and they liked the acting. What they did not like was this refined lady who sat in front of them and who held forth on drama in an absurd accent during the entire interval.

'All the same,' said one, 'she was very refined.'

'Was she?' another asked, 'and is it refined to twitch and scratch I pray?'

There was no immediate answer forthcoming. None of the party was an authority on the precise requirements of the genuinely refined lady. I seized the opportunity to enlighten them with regard to twitching. I quoted Dylan Thomas:

Oh what can I do? I'll never be refined if I twitch .

We may take it then that scratching and twitching are not refined. To be refined is to sit without adjusting buttocks and legs, without twitching, scratching, wriggling, squirming, until you get home when you can scratch at will and squirm and wriggle and make all the noises you like but you must never be caught and that's one of the chief secrets of being successfully genteel.

To be successfully genteel is to be publicly refined. The bother is that if we successfully refine ourselves there is nothing common left and we desperately need commonality if we are to survive in the harsh world around us. We need to merge with other commonplace folk. We need to subside into the crude pudding of humanity.

I remember once in a pub in London one man turned on another and shouted fiercely at him.

'You sir,' he said, 'are not a gentleman.'

Luckily for all of us, the man who was at the receiving end regarded the accusation as a compliment.

'Thanks be to God,' he said, 'sure if I was a gentleman I'd hardly know myself.'

Oddly enough he was one of the most refined chaps I ever met. He did not look in the least refined but he had an art for not giving offence or taking offence and he could deflect awkward questions the way the late Jack Johnson could deflect wild swipes from pretenders to his crown. I think the reason he was referred to as a non-gentleman in the first place was that he started to successfully chat up the barmaid who had earlier repelled the advances of the man who accused him of not being a gentleman.

I'll never be refined. Too many modifications are required for real refinement and I can't afford to be modified expressly, having already been well-modified by a cruel world over the years. The world will not refine you if you meet it head on. It will make you more sensible and it will modify you but refine you, no.

Refinement, alas, can frequently be off-putting and I once heard a bride-to-be described as being too refined to go into a bath naked. It was never revealed how she went into a bath but certainly not in her birthday suit. Anyway there is only room for so many refined people in the world so if you are not refined you should not worry. You belong to the vast majority.

It's a rather odd thing though that refined women frequently marry totally unrefined men and if you don't believe me all you have to do is look around you. You'll seldom if ever see a refined man with a refined woman.

There was another lady of my acquaintance who never went to mass in the body of the church. She was always to be found in the seats far 'from the madding crowd's ignoble strife'. Other women, unrefined, also hear Mass in the sacristy. These are frequently claustrophobic, catarrhous, contrary or even condescending but it has to be said that the majority have valid reasons.

The Ram of God and Other Stories

You will very rarely see refined women at football matches and I wonder if they should be blamed when you consider the strong language so frequently heard when the referee makes a dicey decision. You may frequently observe two refined females together in public and you may even see three on occasion but you will never see more because refined females, like herons, never appear in flocks.

While Stocks Last

There have been some great questions and answers relating to the licensing trade in various towns and villages all over the country but I'm sure I'll be forgiven if I highlight three from my native county and in so doing I would like to remind readers how mindful I am of the natural wit and repartee of other places.

The most famous of the three refers, as one would expect, to that great bastion of life, liberty and the pursuit of happiness which is referred to on maps and signposts as Ballybunion, so called because it was a stronghold of the O'Bannions who, in turn, were watch-dogs for the O'Connors, lords of the Barony.

It transpired in those halcyon days when there was a more liberal view taken of licensing transgressions than there is now that there happened to be a member of the garda síochána standing with his hands behind his back outside the Castle Hotel. The time was a summer's night, in the middle of July and it wanted but three minutes to the witching hour. Up the street there staggered a gentleman who had been asked to vacate a premises on the main thoroughfare. He was, to put it mildly, somewhat annoyed. Truculently he addressed himself to the minion of the law.

'Tell me guard,' said he, 'what time do the pubs close in Ballybunion?'

'After Listowel Races sir,' came the mild answer.

Then there was the night in the village of Duagh which is a historic and delightful spot lying halfway

73

between the towns of Listowel and Abbeyfeale. The carnival was in full swing when a brother and I arrived from our native town, having been informed by a relative from the area that there was an extension in the public houses of Duagh on the night in question because of the carnival. Alas there were some conflicting rumours. A local dignitary advised us that as far as he knew there was no extension, that it was business as usual with closing time at ten o'clock.

'However,' said he, 'you would be well advised to play it by ear and keep an eye open for the Squad.'

By Squad, of course, he meant members of the garda síochána who sometimes on Sunday nights would conduct raids on licensed premises and who sometimes would not. Some publicans insisted that the guards were affected by the moon and were, therefore, unpredictable while other publicans would testify that guards were merely acting on instructions from a higher authority such as a sergeant or a superintendent.

Anyway the brother and I happened to find ourselves on the premises of the late and great Dermot O'Brien who was to Duagh what the Caesars were to Rome.

'Tell me Mister O'Brien,' my brother addressed himself to Dermot who happened to be on duty behind the counter, 'how long more will the pub be open?'

'This pub,' said Dermot O'Brien, 'will be open while stocks last.'

Then there was the night in Killarney after a Munster football final. The pubs were cleared on time. It had been an exhausting day and the publicans were weary from it all. A lone guard stood outside a local hostelry as the crowds departed. Up the street came two Corkmen who had just polished off a steak and chips in one of the town's numerous hostelries and who now needed something intoxicating to assist with the meal's digestion. They had tried several public houses but all in vain.

Wearily they eyed the lone member of the Force, a stoutish chap in his fifties with long years of unblemished service behind him.

'Tell us,' said the leading Corkman, 'do you know where two fellows would get a drink around here?'

'No,' said the custodian of the peace, 'but I know where three fellows would get one.'

Potentates

It happened on Thursday evening last. The normal Thursday patrons were all seated in their rightful places, the same ones they occupied every Thursday. They were unemployed but that's not a sin no more than it was when I was a boy. Thursday was dole day. I might have started in ballad form. For instance:

> *It was on a Thursday evening*
> *And the month it was July*
> *Peace and happiness did reign*
> *And the sun shone in the sky.*

Actually the sun didn't shine but I could find nothing to rhyme with July under the particular set of rules which governed the stanza in question. As a matter of fact it mattered not whether the sun shone or was hidden by cloud. It has no bearing on our story.

There they were, the unemployed, seated happily as was their wont, their cares temporarily shelved and the glow of the few drinks they had taken beginning to show on their faces. Animation entered their conversation and the dreary world went by unheeded outside the public house door.

Then they entered, a group of four, two men, two women. They were a prosperous-looking outfit, well-dressed and rearing for carebo.

Our friends, the unemployed, ceased their conversation and took stock of the new arrivals. Thursday is a great day in Ireland. On that day, because of the monies dispensed by the state, there is a brief surcease from care and woe and the menfolk may drink a few pints from the modest grants allowed them by their hard-pressed wives. Then there are the bachelors who have no wives to keep an eye on them, who may drink the whole danged lot and suffer the consequences.

Yes indeed! Without doubt Thursday is a great day in Ireland. There's money for a little while and it adds a temporary dignity to the deprived and the out of work.

'Give 'em all a drink!' The order came from the fatter of the two gentlemen who had just entered. His instructions were carried out and four fresh pints graced the counter in no time at all.

The recipients, no forelock touchers or lickspittles these, thanked their benefactor, recomposed their posteriors on their stools, coughed, looked around at the newcomers, re-arranged their buttocks a second time and then addressed themselves to their pints. The heads of these were now of the requisite depth and tone. Time for the first sup.

A mature pint of stout is like a blade of golden corn. There's a time to cut it. Cutting too early or too late can be disastrous. The experienced farmer knows exactly when the corn must be cut and the mature pint-drinker knows when his pint must be drank. Now was the time. Carefully, economically, the heads dipped with uniform action. Elbows bent and silently the black liquid passed down the gullets of the grateful four.

As the evening went by they regaled their benefactors with stories. The less fat of the newcomers had also purchased a drink for the residents.

Camaraderie abounded. A song was sung. The residents looked with regard and respect at these over-weight potentates who dispensed drink so freely. But who were they? Where were they bound? Whence had they come?

It transpired that the newcomers were social wel-fare recipients as well. Potentates they were but only for a day. One had borrowed his brother's car to attend a funeral. His wife had come along because it was her duty but the other pair had only come along for the crack!

Great was the joy of the residents. Their spirits soared. If they had been given green pastures in the vicinity they would have lain down among them. Truly their own had come into their own. Not only had they been served with free drinks but the brotherhood of man had also been served.

It was a great day for unemployed Gaels. One group brought gifts to another. They had shared their fortune, small as it was. Tomorrow, alas, was another day, but meanwhile today was today.

Between them the residents managed to put to-gether the price of a round. What a churl I would have been if I had not responded too!

Hail – but not Farewell

The most remarkable aspect of the recent weather has been the absence of hailstones. Normally this here part of the world would have been host to a hundred showers before November's expiry, whereas, this winter there hasn't been a decent downfall so far. I must confess that I sorely miss the hail.

Of all the driblets and downpours that descend upon us from the heavens the hailstone is my favourite. I like snow, of course, and welcome its seasonal appearance. I like rain because it makes for growth and it washes away the grime and filth and imposes a bright face on town and country, although we must ask ourselves to where it is all washed.

I am no lover of sleet. Sleet reminds me of the man who cannot make up his mind what he is. He's Fianna Fáil one minute and he's Fine Gael the next. Sleet has an identity problem.

I confess that every man has the right to change his mind now and again but it's confusing for everybody when he keeps changing it all the time. You never know where you stand with him. He's not the kind of fellow you'd like to see married to your sister and so I do not grapple sleet to any bosom because I cannot depend on it.

Sleet reminds me too of a chap walking towards the house sombrely dressed in common garb but by the time he reaches your door he's all dressed in white. It's all too much for me. I don't know where I stand with sleet.

With your hailstone now it's different. He'll always knock on your door or your window or your roof before he puts in his appearance. He'll never arrive without advertising himself. I will concede that it's a bit of a shock when a thousand hailstones suddenly beat a deafening tattoo on the bedroom window in the middle of the night but it's a shock that changes instantly to delight because it's the hailstones way of advertising himself, of saying: 'Don't be alarmed. It's only me. I mean no harm, just out on a bit of a spree. Won't be staying long. I'll be gone before you know. Just decided to knock and remind you that I am alive and well.'

What he says is true for the hailstone never stays long. He has too many other places to visit. For me there is always something reassuring about a decent shower of hail. There's no harm in hail. A good shower brightens and whitens the landscape but not for long. Therefore, you will appreciate my concern about the decline in hailstone numbers.

If some of your dearest friends were suddenly to disappear without trace wouldn't you be concerned? Wouldn't you be tempted to notify the gardaí? Of course you would, but tell me this. Who do we notify when hailstones disappear?

The other night in the pub a man explained that the disappearance of hail was due to the warming of the climate.

'If it gets any warmer,' he cautioned, 'all the hailstones will disappear. This is only the beginning,' he went on, 'sea levels are rising and so are temperatures.'

I moved out of earshot. Inevitably he would move on to the dwindling size of eggs and that would be too much for me.

The Ram of God and Other Stories

I used to like Gerard Manley Hopkins until he made his famous all-out attack on hailstones. I like to call it 'The Day Hopkins Walked Out On Hail'. The followers of Hopkins will shake their heads in disbelief but his abhorrence of the innocent hailstone is to be found in every treasury in the whole world. Remember:

> *I have desired to go*
> *Where springs not fail,*
> *To fields where flies no sharp and sided hail*
> *And a few lilies blow.*

Nonsensical talk this. Without hail there might not be sufficient water for his springs that do not fail. Did he ever think of that I wonder! Without water there cannot be springs and without springs there cannot be streams and so forth and so on. Hopkins goes on in beautifully paced lines:

> *Where no storms come,*
> *Where the green swell is in the havens dumb,*
> *And out of the swing of the sea.*

Where no storms come eh! If you don't have storms you don't have rain and that would leave us with no spring at all and we'd all die from the drought.

Blind as Hopkins was in respect of hail he's only trotting after our great friend Tennyson. Take for instance 'Morte d'Arthur' where he longs to be in the island valley of Avalon:

> *Where falls not hail, or rain, or any snow*
> *Nor ever wind blows loudly.*

81

This is where he wishes to be and pray will somebody tell me what he's going to do for drinking water if there's no hail or rain or snow. Suppose, for instance, they wished to brew a drop of beer, beloved of all poets, how in God's name would they make it without water? Or is this what is called poetic license? Give me a seven-day license any time.

Shelley, of course, compensates in some small measure when he writes:

> *Hail to thee blithe spirit!*
> *Bird thou never wert,*
> *That from Heaven, or near it,*
> *Pourest thy full heart*
> *In profuse strains of unpremeditated art.*

Some critics will argue that the 'Hail' in this instance is a salutation. I do not agree. If it was any other poet I might go along but is it not Shelley who wrote:

> *I wield the flail of the flashing hail*
> *And whiten the green plains under*
> *And then again I dissolve it in rain*
> *And laugh as I pass in thunder.*

Therefore, we may safely conclude, seeing his regard for hail and rain, that he was wishing the skylark a shower of hail. Skylarks love hail. If they did not they would not spend so much time out of doors.

I accept that a belt of a fair-sized hailstone would floor the average skylark provided it hit him on the head as he was going up and the hailstone coming down. It is well known, however, that skylarks are never airborne when hail is falling. They are grounded by instincts older than poetry. Poetry is a relatively recent development whereas the skylark has been singing for aeons.

When I started this little treatise I cherished faint hopes that there would be a shower of hail before I finished but although the skies darkened not a single hailstone assailed my window. I am, therefore, more concerned at the end of this piece than I was at the start. The future of the hailstone is at stake here, the future that is, of the natural hailstone. There will always be artificial hailstones but you can have those.

> *Oh for a shower of hailstones round and white*
> *To storm my window panes with all its might*
> *Be certain I would rise and sweetly toast*
> *The rapid, raking, rampant, running host.*

Proverbs

Recently I found an old exercise book which belonged to my late father. In the very last page was a collection of proverbs. The fact that he was a schoolmaster all of his life may have influenced his choices and I don't know whether he made the selection on his own behalf or on behalf of his pupils. All told there were one hundred and eighty and each was accorded so many ticks. The best were awarded three, the second best two and the ordinary only one. All made sense however. The first to receive three ticks should make us ponder – 'Our last garment is made without pockets'.

The test of a worthwhile proverb lies in the number of meanings or interpretations which may be drawn from it. Many may be drawn from the following – 'One enemy is too many and a hundred friends too few'. It's from the German and it should teach us that its folly to make enemies when we might easily make friends. The bother arises when we make friends with those who do harm instead of good. Still its better to convert a man to friendship if such a thing is possible. Would this have worked with Hitler or Stalin however?

Now here's a biting one that begs comment – 'Old age, though despised, is coveted by all'.

Here's a sad one but how true alas – 'Old men go to death; death comes to young men'.

Here's another one all the way from the fourteenth century – 'Of little meddling comes great ease'. Ah how very true! I have always maintained that we should not concern ourselves with what others are doing but should be getting on with what we have to do ourselves. I have seen loaves of bread go up in smoke because women preferred watching the antics of their neighbours and I have seen marriages crumble because the combatants showed more interest in marriages other than their own.

And now here's one about Northampton where I once worked although not at the trade which is mentioned. 'Northampton,' says the proverb, 'stands on other men's legs'. Why wouldn't it! Isn't it the centre of the boot trade! Their soccer team goes by the name of the Cobblers and for all their plenitude of boots they have never been in the first division as we know it.

In the long run it's hard to beat the Greeks when it comes to a decent proverb. How about this for a sage observation – 'Nature has given us two ears and two eyes but it has only given us one tongue so that we should hear and see more than we speak'. There's another way of putting it – 'More have repented speech than silence'.

While I am no handwriting expert it is easy enough to deduce that my father collected these proverbs over a long period. The early recordings are made in pen and ink and the later in biro. Also the earlier are more faded than the later. He draws from many sources but there is one of his own – 'Life is funny and life is short but it would be a damn sight funnier if it was any longer'.

My grandmother used to say, God be good to her, that it was bad to be too sweet. The Italians had a better way of putting it – 'Be all honey and the flies will consume you'.

'Lose one hour in the morning and you'll be all day

hunting for it'. How true! I have always found it impossible to recover morning hours or money loaned to a man with a faulty memory. I am the reverse with loaned books. I cannot remember to whom I lent them and am consequently out hundreds.

Here is another risque one – 'Joan is as good as my lady in the dark'. Might I add that no doubt so are Jenny and Jane and Julie, Sally and Sue and you know who.

And what about this for a heartless scoundrel, all the way from the sixteenth century and French to boot – 'It is no more pity to see a woman weep than see a goose go bare-foot'.

And how about this for a home-made one – 'It is high time to coin your own proverbs when others run out'.

Now for one that's not included in my father's list although there are many with the same meaning. It comes from Dan Paddy Andy O'Sullivan the great Renagown matchmaker. Pensions' officers were the bane of Dan's life since the day he applied for and received the blind pension.

'If,' said Dan, 'there is one man that don't look like a pensions' officer that man is a pensions' officer'.

Bingo and the In-Laws

Kitchen infighting seems to be on the decline. Circumstances, of course, have greatly changed and sparring
females no longer find themselves face to face all day.
These would consist of mother-in-law and daughter-in-
law, of sisters-in-law and very often of any two opposing females under the same roof.

In-law incontinence between sisters-in-law, however, used to be the worst of all and I am greatly relieved to be able to say that it is declining. I have always
said that there should be some sort of warning sign on
all the approaches where known in-law antagonists
reside. A simple sign such as IN-LAW OUTBREAK
HERE might be the most effective and economic or you
could have DANGEROUS IN-LAWS AHEAD.

The reasons for its decline are numerous. I would
list the availability of one-person housing as very high,
likewise the increase in homes for old people but most
of all, in my estimation, would be that great game of
chance known as Bingo.

Bingo is the safety valve of all dangerous in-law situations. Before it there was no respite, no escape hatch.
There was simply no place to go after the churches
closed for the night. There were neighbours but neighbours, no matter how compassionate, have only so
much tolerance and they very often require their
households for the solving of their own personal prob-
lems.

It's a mercy indeed that warring females can be

presently accommodated by a more enlightened society which seemed to be once totally ignorant of the fact that friction from morning till night was slowly but surely exterminating reason in so many households.

It wasn't half as bad in the towns as it was in the country places, particularly in the more isolated places. In the town the warring parties could visit the church, the cinema or simply slip out next door just to be away from each other and when the patience of those next door wore out there was always the house on the other side and when the patience there ran out there were other houses manned by friends and relations on side streets, main streets and lanes. Indeed in many houses the visitors would be welcome since they would serve as temporary peace catalysts if there was in-law trouble in the houses they might be visiting.

Words rather than weapons were most used in all affrays although some people would have us believe that words are the worst weapons of all, leaving scars that can last for years. A sound knowledge of the defects and idiosyncrasies, crimes and general failings of the in-law opposition can be the most deadly form of ammunition and can be fired again and again with elaboration and embellishments.

Somebody said that all is fair in love and war and if this is true it is even more fair between in-laws. Rarely, to the casual visitor, is the evidence of serious in-law struggle between females under the same roof visible to the naked eye. It takes a keen student of this particular type of war to read between the lines as it were. This war has been so vicious and so extended in certain cases that the protagonists have often wished for permanent release from their suffering.

That is why I take off my hat to Bingo. I hear accounts every day of peace and tranquillity in households where the wife and the sister-in-law were constantly at loggerheads. When one departs for a Bingo session there is no fuel left to the other and so peace must reign. In households where the two warring factions go singly to Bingo every second night there is almost constant peace.

I used to knock Bingo for taking away audiences from plays but wasn't that a really classic case of vested interests. I was thinking only of myself or so it must seem. Now I withdraw all I have said. I am all for Bingo, the single greatest mollifier of the in-law syndrome. Where priests and parsons and even bishops have failed, where peace-makers cracked up and neighbours wrung their hands in despair, where husbands and brothers hung their heads in shame Bingo stepped in and conflict stepped out.

I have cited other factors but this great national game has succeeded where even the most eminent psychologists have failed.

Dirha Bog Revisited

The rising moon abandoned the confines of the hill and was imperceptibly ascending the great, blue vault of the heavens. At the left hand side of the goatpath a hovering lark rejoiced. The little creature flew upwards and upwards until the sky seemed to overflow with its trilling mixture of joyous exclamations. I moved onward to a place where there was silence. A blessed calm had descended upon pathways and hedgerows. The singing of the disappearing lark was still to be heard but the outpouring was of such faint proportions that it only fringed the silence with greater emphasis.

In the distance on another pathway, once frequented by goats, two women appeared, their red and yellow dresses brightening the scene. Is there anything sweeter to the male ear than the distant babbling of mature women!

The moon had now made further advances into her cloudless kingdom. She would reign silent and supreme until Aurora lighted the tips of the Stacks Mountains with long fingers of passionate flame.

I never dwell too long on the moon. When I was a boy the old folk used to say that a moonwatcher could become more obsessed with the orb of night than with a beautiful woman. Then there was an uncle of mine who maintained that he was being watched by the moon. That is why he liked clouds so much. 'The sun only singes the head,' said he, 'but the moon singes the brain.' How's that Christopher Fry speaks of the moon in 'The Lady's Not For Burning':

> *The moon is nothing*
> *But a circumambulating aphrodisiac*
> *Divinely subsidized to provoke the world*
> *Into a rising birth-rate.*

'The moon,' my grandmother used to say, 'is only an egg laid by the sun and 'tis the only roundy egg ever laid'.

I came eventually to the furthest extremes of Dirha Bog. From here when the prevailing wind is active one may scent the salty tang of the great Atlantic but alas the rude noises of the roadway intrude. I turned my back on the magnificent vista of Mount Brandon and the attendant range of the Dingle mountains. I turned for home and for a contrasting scenario. Ballygrennane and its adjoining hills dominated the scene.

'We're very grand,' a Ballygrennane woman once informed me, 'we always look down on the people of Listowel.' So well they might and they four hundred feet above us.

Several larks were now singing and far, far away an anxious hound voiced his concern for himself and his master but the moon still ascended her domain, unmoved by the canine plea.

As I neared the end of the bogpath where my car was parked an enchanted, white mist began to rise from the encroaching fields. I came to the disused railway line and paused to bid farewell to my bogland paradise. Then a strange thing happened. I found myself putting my hand into my trousers pocket where I keep my money. I extracted some notes and looked around for someone to pay. There should have been an attendant present in peaked cap with a money satchel across his shoulders and a ticket dispenser in his hand. My money still in my hand I looked everywhere but there was nobody to be seen save a hunting tomcat.

'Imagine,' I said to the cat, 'it's all for nothing, not a single penny to be paid after the most wonderful evening for which one could wish.' I had it all, unlimited lark music, a setting sun and a rising moon, vistas that absolutely baffle description and air as pure as could be found anywhere in the wide world.

I returned my money to my pocket for the truth was not so much that the best things in life are free but if I were to put all my possessions together there would not be sufficient to pay for all that I had seen and all that I had experienced that evening on the vast boglands of Dirha.

Ankles Etcetera

The argument still rages as to whether the ankles or the buttocks are the more engaging aspects of a woman's make-up. Personally I score it about fifty/fifty but, oddly enough, the majority of my readers would seem to favour the ankle over the posterior. I haven't conducted a poll or anything like that but I have re-ceived over twenty letters since I first wrote about the subject of female posteriors and I can tell you that I would not have opted for such a subject at all if I thought it would create so much controversy.

As much as some men admire the contours of the female posterior they rhapsodise altogether when it comes to a pair of ankles. Take this letter from the ancient city of Cork, name and address supplied.

'What a base fellow you are,' it opens, 'and I always thinking that J.B. Keane was a proper aesthete. Now I find that you place the posterior ahead of the ankle. Only the ignorant and the backward would place the female posterior before a female ankle. There is nothing my dear scribe as delicate as a well-turned ankle. No artist, not even Michael Angelo, could do justice to a female ankle whereas every lavatory defiler in every country of the world has drawn a posterior on the walls of 'the throneroom of soliloquy' as you once called a gents toilet. I'm afraid J.B. that you give yourself away and I, for one, will hold you suspect for evermore now that I know you can be carried away by a female posterior. Oh weak-willed fellow who promised so much for so long.

'Not even if you were to go around for evermore with an arch made from *agnus castus* over your head would I believe that you were the chaste chappie you once seemed to be.'

There is more but I think that 'Corkonian' as he calls himself has made his point. I must deny, regretfully, having coined the phrase, the throneroom of soliloquy. The credit for this choice item of classic descriptiveness must go to the late and great Lisselton poet Robert Leslie Boland or Bob Boland as he was popularly known. As for the *agnus castus* I had better enlighten my reader having been enlightened myself by the family dictionary, now sixty-three years old and still going strong.

The *Agnus Castus* is a shrub of the verbena family, a native of the Mediterranean countries and is supposed to preserve chastity. We are grateful to 'Corkonian' for adding to our store of knowledge but not so grateful to him for presuming that yours truly was ever carried away by a female posterior. While I admire this blessed object as much as the next man I am not obsessed with it. Neither am I obsessed by ankles but with the female as a whole, yes I am rightfully obsessed and truly appreciative.

As far as I know there has never been a major poem written about an ankle or a pair of ankles. In fact I cannot recall any sort of poem on the subject. The word curvaceous, however, appears a thousand times in major poems and we may take it that the word applies not to ankles but to female posteriors.

The only derogatory reference to posteriors that I can recall came from Dan Paddy Andy O'Sullivan the great matchmaker, himself a man with a profound appreciation of female rears since he was asked on a regular basis to describe the particular areas of the female anatomy for aspiring husbands. Dan once said that nothing wiggled like a female posterior and nothing stood out like it.

Alas when he was asked by the father of the bride-to-be to describe the land on the farm where she would be spending the rest of her life Dan replied that she would only be up to her ankles in it.

'Worse,' said Dan, 'if she was up to her bum in it.'

This is the only instance I know of where the ankle takes precedence over the posterior.

Shakespeare, in *Love's Labour Lost*, has this to say

In the posteriors of this day;
Which the rude multitude call the afternoon.

Shakespeare has nothing to say about ankles but I hold the ankle in no less esteem for this.

It is, my friends, all a matter of attitude. What is one man's food is another man's poison and those who loathe posteriors may well love ankles. All I'm asking for is moderation of attitude. Do not consign to the ash can that which you cannot appreciate. In short, do not demean the gentle posterior simply because you may have ankles on the brain.

Cuckoos and Canvassers

That blessed bird of the twin notes, the Moroccan cuckoo failed to show up this year in Dirha Bog, once the home of Canavan's great goat herd, numerous pheasants and mallard, owls, bats and curlews, crested plovers and snipe, believe it or not for a brief period, and one wild pig. This dangerous and disorderly female of the porcine species was once domesticated but forsook Canavan's croteen for the joys and freedom of bogland life, glutting herself with frogs, field mice, rats and even stoats as well as raiding farmhouses for miles around whenever the natural food supply ran out.

She was executed on the 15 August after she killed and consumed a young greyhound worth ten times more dead than he could ever hope to be alive. Jack Duggan wrote a verse about his passing but the words escape me. I'll have to have a chat with his daughter Philly who still resides with her husband and family in her beloved Dirha. Maybe there's a copy somewhere.

Sigerson Clifford, the Cahirsiveen poet also wrote about a rogue pig who hailed from the townland of Coonaclyre contiguous to his native town. After many adventures this murderous swine ended his days in that most musical of villages, Scartaglin. Here is how Clifford describes the events leading up to his demise:

They trapped him for a circus den
But soon the news went round
That he killed and ate a tiger
Worth a hundred pounds.

They killed him then in Scartaglin
And there he did expire,
Far, far away from all his friends
And the fields of Coonaclyre.

There was also a rogue pig in Listowel, in the late 1930s who was as thin as a whippet and faster than a cheetah. He fed in many houses but he really belonged to none. He committed the unpardonable sin of eating a black biretta which had been left on the window sill of a house in Convent Lane while its priestly wearer went inside to partake of a mug of tea. It was bad enough to devour a tiger and worse to devour a greyhound but the last of all was to devour a priest's hat for this was a sacrilege and being a pig, according to his executioners, was no excuse. They drowned him in a brown flood but rumour had it afterwards that his ghost was seen walking along the banks of the estuary on moonlit nights in the company of seals and sea otters, often with a salmon in his mouth and often when nobody was looking, with a young seal.

This, however, is not why I have come here today. The foregoing was just in passing. My real reason for being here is to bemoan the non-arrival of the cuckoo for the first time in living memory and also to celebrate the arrival of an all-too familiar and welcome replacement, the common or garden political canvasser who has just started to re-appear in town and country in recent days in the run-up to the local elections.

97

The first group so far this year passed me on the road not far from Dirha. The party consisted of five male canvassers and one female. They moved silently but not solemnly as was their wont in former times. Their car was parked in the suburbs of the town and they were covering the houses which stood between Listowel and Dirha.

I waved fondly at them as I passed but there was no responding wave. I belonged to a different party from the one which they represented and I was, therefore, not worth wasting a wave on. They would call to my house all right in the line of duty knowing that they had as much hope of my vote as I would have of theirs had I contested the election.

I admire canvassers. They neither expect nor receive payment for their work. They can absorb all the abuse and all the complaints showered upon them throughout the campaign. If their candidate loses they are blamed for not doing their job properly, for not being respectable enough or not conversely down-to-earth enough, for being too drunk or too sober, for being too serious or too capricious, too banal or too flippant. They cannot win but those they champion sometimes do. An election without canvassers would be, in my estimation, like a plate of corned beef without cabbage or a smile without teeth in it. Extend a welcome then to all canvassers or else he too may disappear from the suburbs of Listowel like the cuckoo.

Posterior Patting I

A serious letter from a woman who informs me that there is a man in her place of employment who pats female posteriors all the time. They are not pats of a lingering nature but she maintains that a posterior pat is still a posterior pat and, as such, must be regarded as a violation of womanhood. He does not follow up the patting procedure with touches of a more advanced nature – 'and,' says she, 'I'd say this is why nobody takes much notice of him. His face was slapped once or twice and he was kicked in the shin but there was no complaint of sexual harassment. He patted me on the Thursday evening before the most recent weekend and I shouted at him.

'How dare you!' I said and he seemed about to collapse at my reaction. He turned a ghastly pale and then moved off.'

The letter goes on to say that she regards the practice of posterior-patting as despicable. I agree completely and I must concede that any man who pats a female posterior without a proprietor's permission is nothing short of a cad and should have his own posterior soundly kicked although, would you believe, when I discussed this very topic with a number of women one night recently, the oldest of the group said that it was merely a sign of health.

''Tis only a sign of health,' said she much to the chagrin of her listeners who roundly condemned the practice.

'If a fella did it to me,' said one of the younger, more mettlesome members of the company, 'I'd split him.'

There were mumblings of approval so I would ask would-be posterior patters to take note. When I read this woman's letter I was undecided as to whether I should discuss this disputatious subject or not but then I told myself that every man born of woman is a potential patter.

I'll put it another way. Any given man is capable of patting any given female posterior at any given time. Such is the nature of man that not even the most outwardly reliable, the most spiritual, even the most disciplined is capable of suddenly transforming himself into a posterior-patter. Don't ask me what triggers off the impulse to pat. I simply don't know. It has led to serious trouble, even violence, from time to time, and yet this odious practice goes on. Slipping a reassuring and friendly hand around a female waist is more or less acceptable but let the object of the palm's descent be a few inches further down and the entire ball game is changed. Several men with whom I discussed the topic were reluctant to air their views but all were agreed that a lingering pat was an invasion of a lady's privacy and that the perpetrator should be punished.

'It is an eminently pattable object,' one of the gentle-men with whom I discussed the subject was heard to say, 'but,' he continued with a wagging forefinger, 'pattable and all that it is, it must not be patted and that is that. No harm at all,' he continued, 'to pat the posterior of your partner but the patting of a mere acquaintance is criminal. Patting a complete stranger is a recipe for self-destruction especially if she is in the company of her own personal posterior patter, to wit her lifelong love and custodian and partner and wedded husband.'

'Posterior patting,' said another man, this time a middle-aged chap, 'is an act of impurity and I say this in the knowledge that my age group is possessed of more potential posterior patters than any other.'

Some listeners disagreed with him. They were of the considered opinion that the older a man is the more likely he is to pat.

I must say on a personal note however that tempting as it is the urge must be resisted at all costs for the good reason that the vast majority of women find it offensive and the handful who don't, as the man said, are not worth patting.

To the woman who triggered all this off through the medium of her letter I have this to say. Thank you for your epistle and my advice is that you should resist, as you have been doing all along, the primitive urges of all posterior patters regardless of their age or position.

Calumny

I once listened spellbound in a public house to as sustained and as damaging a battery of calumny as was ever heard between the so-called four walls of this world or, indeed, ever heard in any port or any ship that faced the four winds on any of the seven seas. The victim of this seemingly unprovoked attack was well-known to me. I had always regarded him as a decent oul' skin, totally harmless and in fact without either the guile or the malice to do harm to anybody. Yet here he was, being consigned by a friend and neighbour to the very bottom of the heap which, when you take the varied crimes of mankind into account, is simply not the place to be.

The man with whom I was drinking bade me to be still when I would rush to the defence of the calumniated. 'Hush you fool,' said he, ''tis only politics.'

So there we have it. No notice whatsoever must be taken when one man annihilates the character of another because of his politics. Politics brings out the worst in certain individuals. They will not see the good in their brothers because those very same brothers are of a different political persuasion.

As we listened to the on-going calumny I felt obliged to agree with my friend who had cautioned me to remain silent. Indeed it would seem that no man could be half as bad as the calumniated man. We were told that he was a backbiter and a wasp, a jackass who couldn't lace his boots and as mean a wretch as ever dodged his legitimate round in a public house.

All of this took place a long time ago but nothing much has changed in the interim. The calumny has become more savage but hides have also thickened proportionately.

In that distant time it was different. By all the laws I should not have been in the pub for two reasons. The first is that I was under age and the second is that it was after hours. I must say here, however, that nobody minded the under-age drinker in those days. If he could put it back and retain it, as well as conduct himself properly, nobody minded. What they really minded was the over-age drinker who became drunk because he couldn't take it.

As the calumniator continued with his tirade we heard that the calumniated was not only a born troublemaker but that he piddled in the bed as well and all this because he had the temerity to put forward his name as a candidate in the county council elections. If he had not entered he would have been the fine fellow he always was.

Just when we thought the barrage was about to conclude the calumniator swallowed the meagre contents of his depleted whiskey glass and finally declared that the new candidate was nothing but a bloody masturbator. This drew gasps and even my companion, a man of the world, was shocked. However, it was myself who was the most shocked of all.

Earlier that year I had attended a school's mission at the end of which I was shrived of my transgressions by the missioner and sent forth into the world a purer and a more redoubtable Catholic. I remembered with horror how the missioner had held us enthralled while he spoke of the evils of masturbation. It transpired that he had been in the east end of London one afternoon visiting a home for the elderly and dying when he beheld an old man in the corner of a ward given to no-hopers. The old fellow signalled the missioner who went over at once to listen to the dying man.

'He's only twenty-five,' a nurse informed the man of God.

'But he looks ninety,' said that worthy as he bent to hear out the miserable creature on the bed. The poor fellow was hard put to express himself according to the missioner. He puked and he groaned. His eyes rolled and sloshed in their sockets as he tried to form words which would explain his case. Finally he seized the missioner's hand and gasped out the words: 'I was a masturbator,' he spluttered through clenched teeth and then he fell out of the bed with a diabolical screech before expiring on the floor of the ward.

The moral inferred by the missioner was that we young students might well end up the same way.

Meanings

Now we'll talk about meanings. For meanings you may deduce that we are treating with how we should interpret certain communications. If we are to interpret properly we must listen carefully. Let me illustrate. There is an ancient saying still prevalent in the Irish countryside which goes as follows:

'I know what you mean all right sir but the grass is wet'.

I know what it means and so do most of the older generation but just in case you don't, let me elaborate. The statement, quite obviously, was made by a gentleman to a maid. He was, apparently, a man of higher station as they used to say in those days. Otherwise she would not have called him sir. We must take it that the gentleman in question made an improper suggestion to the maid and that she declined on the grounds that the grass was wet. This, of course, means that they met out of doors and that a shower of rain had just passed. Otherwise how would the grass be wet. I suspect, however, that the grass was not wet at all but that the young lady, rather than offend a person of higher station, blamed the wet grass for the fact that she could not accommodate him. It happens all the time. The meaning that the rejected party must draw from the unqualified refusal is that the lady might be willing in other circumstances.

I was once taken aback when a married couple arrived at my premises one night many years ago.

They were what we refer to as respectable, solid, well-got, well-disposed, religious, loyal and true. The male of the partnership was possessed of a sense of humour while the female presented a somewhat austere picture.

No sooner had he seated his partner than he arrived at the bar counter. 'For myself,' said he, 'there will be a pint of stout and for my missus there will be a double leg-opener.'

I nodded and proceeded with the filling of the pint. As the glass filled I tried in vain to identify the other part of the order. I must confess that certain ideas came to me but I dismissed these instantly because they were not of the variety that one would associate with the prim wife who sat sedately awaiting the return of her husband.

A large leg-opener! I repeated the phrase to myself several times and wondered if it was some new form of cocktail or had new cider been released on to the market unknown to me. To further ponder the situation I allowed the pint to settle and intimated to our friend that the night was a fine one and that the prospects looked good.

'The wind is from a good quarter,' he said.

After some further exchanges I handed him his pint hoping that I would be enlightened about the constituents of the large leg-opener.

'What about my vodka?' he asked. So there it was. The large leg-opener was no more than a large vodka. However we view the matter it has to be conceded in the end that the man's motives were legitimate although, if pressed, the wife might concede that all she asked for was a small vodka.

Once with a friend I arrived at a hotel in Cork city.

Already late for an appointment we thrust our bags into the outstretched hands of Tom the porter.

'Book us in,' I told him, 'and we'll see you later.'

'Dass awright Mister Keane boy,' Tom assured me.

'Wasn't that a bit forward,' my friend suggested as we hurried to our appointment.

'It could have been less forward,' I informed him. Then I went on to explain that Tom and I were old acquaintances. In saying 'dass awright Mister Keane boy' he was being both respectful and affectionate at the same time. It's a delicate mix but it's common in that lovely city by the Lee. When a Corkman calls you boy he's really calling you brother. Tom's assurance to me was also paternal. When he said, 'Dass all right Mister Keane boy' he was really saying 'that's all right oul' son' and he was as far from being derogatory as the Cape of Good Hope is from Gurranebraher.

107

Language with a Lilt

I once overheard the following words when I was a garsún in the Stacks Mountains – 'The reason he didn't marry up to now was that no one would have him, not even the Hag Hanafin and she gone seventy-nine this Shrove with a whisker around her mouth like a furze bush in a gap and the bare pinch of hair on her poll like a plume on a pilibín.'

A pilibín, of course, is a crested plover, one of the more beautiful feathered visitors from Scandinavia, arriving in late autumn and departing in early spring.

But back to the words I heard; you'd never hear language like that now. It was the kind of speech that flourished in the Stacks particularly the Renagown area in the pre-telephone, pre-television years.

There was a retired policeman living in peace there when I was a growing boy. He was once offered a sandwich by a Tralee man who happened to be cutting turf with a party of friends in Carraigcannon. He refused but not without proffering a reason: 'What is a sandwich,' said he, 'but two barely-buttered slices of bread concealing the dietary inadequacies of that which lies between them?'

But what about the man who was turned down by the Hag Hanafin? How did he fare in the marriage stakes in the end?

Dan Paddy Andy, the great late matchmaker, found a partner for him.

'First,' said he, 'you must get out the black teeth

and get in the white. Get yourself barbered and oiled and stunk (perfumed) and she'll make for you the first night like a cow making for aftergrass.'

Then there was a returned priest who once described an area nearer Tralee which was almost denuded of people, in the following terms: 'If I could personify this part of rural Ireland,' said he, 'I would see it as an unshaven unfortunate wearing a long black coat and a cap. He would be standing at the door of a public house in Tralee with porter stains around his mouth and a bloodstained parcel of boiling beef under his oxter. He would be futilely waving after the last bus to his native place. In short he has missed the bus of life and now he must struggle home on his own.'

Then there was the time an elderly bachelor arrived at Dan Paddy Andy's residence in Renagown looking for a wife, not too old or too young but nice and firm, his own words. A listener proceeded to cronawn asserting that the fellow was too old to be entertaining notions about marriageable women.'

'Listen,' said Dan, 'if you saw two asses coupling would you question the age of the stallion or would you deny him his share of the natural joys of the world? If you saw a pair of crows threading,' Dan went on, 'would you ask the cock for his birth certificate?'

'You would not,' said Dan, 'but you'd deny a Christian.'

Posterior Patting II

Letters go leor now on the subject of posterior patting. Most of the letters written by females disapprove strongly and insist that unprovoked posterior patting by the male of the species is one of the viler forms of sexual harassment.

On the other hand a number of letters from older women take a more lenient view. One writes:

Dear John B.,

I am a married woman now in my seventy-third year. I am happily married. Next door to me there was a man, now deceased, and there wasn't a day that he didn't give me a pat. He'd be leaving at night after a chat and he would always manage to get his pat in, unseen by all. That's as far as it went. There were twenty-eight years of it altogether. There was never more than the bare pat. To tell you the truth I miss him, not the pat but himself. He was a good neighbour and there are worse faults.

Name and address is supplied.

There is a letter from a man who calls himself an unrepentant patter. 'That's what they are there for,' he writes, 'so whenever I see a pattable posterior I pat. There are some which are not sufficiently inviting.'

This letter becomes somewhat maudlin and gives an account of the posturing indulged in by some females in order that a pat or pats might be forthcoming. The writer concedes that only a minority of females invite pats. He also maintains that there is nothing as lonely in the world as a female whose behind was never patted by the hand of man.

Another man writes, an unmarried man this time. 'To pat or not to pat,' he writes, 'that is the question whether 'tis nobler in the mind to take up arms against a sea of bottoms and, by opposing, pat them. But when the pat is done what trials will come. Aye, there's the rub, sorry the pat.'

A lady from Corbally writes to say that she used to visit a shop in downtown Limerick for years until one morning the owner came from behind the counter and patted her behind for no reason whatsoever.

'How dare you,' I said to him, and walked out of the shop never to come back. I heard later that he wasn't that kind of man at all and I often wonder what got into him. I still feel guilty although I know that I shouldn't.'

'Posterior patting is a science,' writes a man who supplies name and address and indeed is quite well known to me.

'You have heard of the expression, the patter of little feet,' he writes. 'Well now for a change here is a patter of little bottoms. On no account would I attempt to pat a large posterior. If a small woman objects and draws a clout the effect is not too serious but if a woman of twelve or thirteen stone lands one you could be maimed for life.'

Now comes what I believe to be the most practical letter of the lot. It is written by a secondary teacher of nearly forty years experience And who, praise to the Lord, says she is a fan of mine for thirty years.

'Now,' she writes, 'the subject of posterior patting

which you raised so sensitively recently, often comes up in class, particularly with sixth years and I always advise the girls that you must never turn your back on a man when alone with him because a man is no more than a wild animal and when we know this we are forearmed. Also it is well to remember that every man is a potential patter and it doesn't pay to fall for the charms or the guiles which men use for all the wrong reasons. To escape patting the best course is to position oneself properly so as to give the potential patter no chance. Let there be distance always between the patter and the potential victim and let there be caution when leaving. This is when most pats occur. Some men think they are entitled to a farewell pat when saying good-bye to a woman. They have no such right. I have found publicans and grocers angling themselves for pats more so than other walks of life but I have always been too fast off my feet.'

There is a good deal more but I feel that this good lady has made her point. There would seem to me to be a need for a handbook which would set out the pitfalls of patting. I have no doubt it would be a best-seller so over to you who have been patted and have pity on the patted-to-be.

Fill 'Em Up Again

And now a tale from the world of natural theology. It concerns a chap who lived contiguous to the beautiful town of Ballybunion. He is long since departed the scene, poor fellow. But make no mistake about it, he presently resides in heaven for he was a goodly type with few faults although if taking an extra pint or two is a fault he must be faulted.

However, we are not here to argue Canon Law.

There he was, poor fellow, seated in Mikey Joe's Irish-American Bar of a summer's afternoon, without a care in the world. In front of him on the counter sat a freshly-filled pint of stout. As he sat, deep in happy thought, who should enter the premises but an American damsel with a fine figure and a handsome face. She was far from being tender in years but we won't hold that against her. I am one who believes that a woman isn't fully blossomed until she is fifty at least. Other eminent authorities would be quick to agree with me.

She sat on a stool, placed her handbag on the counter in front of her and called for a Scotch on the rocks.

'Will you join me, Mister?' she asked Paddy Joe who might not have been possessed of much of the world's riches but was the proprietor of a genuinely priceless asset, an honest face.

Since he had never refused the offer of a drink in his life he decided that it would not be appropriate to start there and then. He told his benefactress that he

113

would have a pint of stout. So saying, he polished off the pint in front of him and awaited the arrival of another.

After three pints, all paid for by the American visitor, she asked if he could sing an Irish song, particularly 'Mother Machree', which she had learned at her mother's knee. Now it so happened that Paddy Joe was possessed of a fine tenor voice and not only did he sing 'Mother Machree' but he also sang 'The Old Bog Road' before eventually massacring 'Danny Boy'. I wonder how many times 'Danny Boy' has been massacred in Ballybunion? Between the pair of them, Paddy Joe and the Yank, they demolished a gallon of porter and the best part of a bottle of Scotch.

Evening arrived and from the nearby church came the ancient and heavenly sound of the Angelus bell. Paddy Joe rose to his feet manfully and recited the Angelus in reverential tones. His American friend responded and they agreed afterwards that they both felt infinitely more spiritual after the recital. In fact they felt downright religious and the Yank told Paddy Joe that she felt ashamed because she hadn't been to confession for several years.

'I'd really love to go,' said she with tears in her eyes.

'Your worries are over,' said Paddy Joe, 'for it just so happens that the parish priest is hearing confessions tonight.'

After another drink Paddy Joe led the way to the church. Confessions were in progress and she took her place on a stool near the box. After a while her turn came and she entered.

Now it so happened that, at the other side, there was a sinner who hadn't darkened the door of a confession box for twenty-five years. He was a long time unloading his cargo.

Meanwhile the Yank waited for the priest to slide the shutter in her box but he was so long in doing so that she began to doze and after a few more minutes, what with the heat of the confessional and the natural heat of the weather, she fell into a gentle sleep. When the parish priest eventually pulled aside the slot she was fast asleep. He coughed and harrumphed and made other discreet sounds to attract her attention and, fin- ally, she awakened in a daze. She had forgotten where she was.

'Well,' said the parish priest, 'and pray, what have you to say for yourself?'

'You can fill 'em up again,' she told him, 'a Scotch on the rocks for me and a pint for Paddy Joe.'

When the priest failed to react positively, she told him to have one himself.

The Wrong Man

Laugh and scoff if you will but there's a lot to be said for matchmaking. I don't mean the marrying of two people who never laid eyes on each other until the morning of the marriage. This kind of marriage has as little chance of success as some of the fly-by-night marriages of today. Although I am all for love at first sight the longer a couple know each other the better. Neither am I on the side of everlasting courtships which were quite common when I was a garsún.

I knew several couples who courted till the day they died but for one reason or another never took the ultimate step. You'd often have an unfortunate girl tied to a doting father who, more often than not, outlived her and you'd often have an unfortunate man whose equally doting parents declined to sign over the farm. Situations like these resulted in everlasting courtships. At least the pair met once a week under a hedge or against the gable of a house and if there was no fulfilment there was always the distant prospect of the same.

Of the four hundred marriages arranged by Dan Paddy Andy O'Sullivan, matchmaker extraordinary, only one was a failure. We won't go into the details except to say that the female of the relationship was dead set against fulfilling her part of the consummation and without consummation marriage is just a gun without ammunition.

We see, therefore, that Dan Paddy Andy's success

rate was nothing short of phenomenal by modern standards. Dan achieved a ninety-nine and three-quarters percent yes vote from those he had joined together although half of the ungrateful creatures didn't pay him for the inestimable services he rendered.

Dan, of course, was always careful to point out that while the marriages were successful there were periods when they were no beds of roses. There were ups and downs naturally but then a marriage without ups and downs is in danger of becoming a very boring affair.

Dan was always strongly opposed to the idea of country girls marrying townies. He rarely gave his blessing to such liaisons claiming that townies should marry townies and leave the country girls alone.

'You see,' said Dan, 'your country boy only goes to town the odd Sunday night or by day for some special occasion whereas your townie is in town the whole time.'

What Dan meant by this was that being in town the townie had regular access to public houses and other places of amusement whereas the country boy was rarely contaminated by such constant exposure to the temptations of the world.

'Your townie,' said Dan, 'can't take two steps but he finds himself outside the door of a public house or a cinema or a dancehall and that's every night of the week. Your country boy is under his quilt before midnight and is well able to work the following day whereas townies does hardly be able to open their eyes. You see there's always some kind of diversion going on in the town.'

Although Dan was a religious enough man he would point out that there was a mission in most towns every year.

'Whereas I may tell you,' said he, 'that country places has to settle for one every seven years and maybe that's enough.'

There was a young lady who was both a neighbour and a friend of Dan's. 'A fine slip of a girl she was,' Dan told us, 'you'd look around on the road after her and there's many a garsún guided his ass or pony into a ditch after she passin'.'

Anyhow it transpired that she fell in love with a townie. According to Dan he had all the classic points of a townie. There were the low shoes or slippers as country folk called them. Then the fellow apparently wore a collar and tie on a continuing basis without having earned the right to wear same. It wouldn't be too bad if he was a schoolteacher or an insurance agent or a warble fly inspector but the fellow hadn't even a job!

Dan would shake his head in horror as he outlined the remainder of the townies characteristics. Rumour had it that the scoundrel shaved every day and was never without a crease in his trousers whether the day was Sunday or Monday and on top of that he was not above using stink, i.e. probably after-shave lotion which was a rarity of rarities at the time. In fact the only time after-shave lotion was smelled in country places was when some emigrant returned from America. On top of all this the townie in question used hair oil the seven days of the week and carried a nail file in his top pocket. This last was felt to be the be-all and end-all of blackguardism. Nail files were all right for film stars but for a townie with no job and a perverse dislike of jobs it was felt that he was outstepping himself. In addition to all this the scoundrel wore white socks, was never done whistling day or night and was, according to Dan Paddy Andy: 'A hoor for cheek to cheek dancing!'

Dan advised the girl to have nothing to do with this particular townie and when that failed he went to the girl's parents.

'There are some townies and they're not too bad,' Dan explained, 'townies that will do an honest week's work and take off their hats and caps to a priest like ourselves but this buck I'm talking about is the worst kind of townie. He won't work. He won't look for work and he won't get up in the mornings.'

The parents promised to do what they could but they were old and all their importuning went for nothing. Other sources claimed that the townie in question was an indoor man by day and an outdoor man by night. That is to say he would spend the day in front of the fire and the night carousing.

Fond as he was of the fire he would never go to the bog. His father cut the turf and his mother helped him with the footing and the drawing-out. However, our poor country girl thought he was the bees' knees. She had never, of course, seen the likes of him before except at the cinema.

In the end she married him and he took her to live with his father and mother. She lived unhappily ever after. Herself and her father-in-law and mother-in-law worked their fingers to the bones to keep the scoundrel in porter and cigarettes and when he arrived from the pub at night if there wasn't a plate of sausages or black-puddings waiting for him there would be bedlam.

He always dressed like a dandy whilst his wife and his mother slunk from house to church in black shawls and told no one about their misery. Luckily he died young from a disease of the liver and after a decent interval his wife returned to her home in the Stacks Mountains. She still retained her looks although there were marks on her face from the beatings she received from her late husband.

In the course of time Dan Paddy Andy went matchmaking for her and found for her, not far from the town of Killorglin, a small farmer. This man was no chicken but he was a sappy for his years. They had several children and do I have to confirm that they lived happily ever after!

Of course they did. Years later Dan met her at the fair of Puck where she told him that she should have listened to him when she was younger.

'No,' Dan told her, 'you listened to your heart which is the right thing to do. Where you went astray was that you met the wrong man.'

Shake Hands with the Devil

There was a man in Ballybunion once who used to catch rabbits by means of snares. He would attach a loop of light copper wire to a small stake and as soon as the rabbit was ensnared there was no escape. The more he struggled the tighter became the snare. The rabbit snarer was an agreeable fellow and for some strange reason he was never accused of cruelty to animals. In fact I never heard or read of a rabbit-snarer who was so maybe it's only the rabbit who thinks it's cruel. Rabbits, like hares, can be unreasonable like that.

Anyway to proceed with our tale the rabbit-snarer was a chap much addicted to strong drink particularly Jamaican rum and bottled beer, a disintegrating diet for all save the strongest stomachs. As soon as he disposed of his rabbits he would entrench himself in his favourite pub and spend his earnings on the aforementioned intake.

When the rabbit money would be spent he would make himself so agreeable to the visiting strangers for which Ballybunion is notorious that they considered it a favour if they were allowed to buy him a drink. Other of his victims would have been local drunkards who found it impossible to hold audiences when they became maudlin'.The rabbit-snarer would listen attentively to all sorts of raimeish and even encourage the drunkards to continue, remarking from time to time how sagacious were their comments. Out of appreciation for his perspicacity they would buy him drinks and he would listen enthralled while they made the most pedestrian of outpourings.

He would hang on until the flow of drink was staunched by self-inflicted impoverishment after which he would cast about him for other sources. The result of this prodigious consumption often left him with shaking hands and trembling eyelids when he woke up in the morning. His judgment was also impaired which left him in no condition for the confrontation of his life which took place on the early morning of 16 August in a graveyard contiguous to Ballybunion. In those days Ballybunion was noted for its mushrooms as well as its rabbits. The rabbit-snarer, in fact, became a mushroom-gatherer during the mushroom season. He would rise with dawn and head for the golflinks where the mushrooms abounded. The earnings from the mushrooms went the same road as the earnings from the rabbits.

One sunny morning on the date cited our friend happened to be passing through the graveyard with two buckets of mushrooms when all of a sudden he was seized by the leg. His heart stopped but fortunately for him it started again. His immediate thought was that someone had risen from the dead and was determined to bring him under. He tried to scream but no sound came. The more he tried to escape the tighter became the grip by the unseen underground hand. Finally he found his voice and there followed a series of roars which would do justice to a three year old bull. Alas and alack it was early in the morning. There was nobody abroad. Terrified to look around at the ghastly visage of the creature who held him fast he fainted. He recovered and again he roared for all he was worth.

All in all he spent some two and a half hours in the grip of the underground demon. At last his weakening cries were heard by a winkle-picker on her way to the shore. She entered the graveyard with considerable trepidation and called from a distance to find out what the matter was.

"Tis the devil,' he called back, 'he has me by the leg.'

'Devil the devil do I see,' said the winkle-picker as she approached. She examined the leg which was held fast and discovered that he thrust his leg in one of his own forgotten rabbit loops. It was a well-made loop. After awhile she managed to release him but to her horror discovered that his hair had turned white.

The moral of this story is that you should never set traps unless you are prepared to fall into one some time. As they say in French; *cela va sans dire*.

Foul Talk

Quite recently I beheld a youngster fling a stone at an old woman as she made her way past the back door of my premises on her way to the post office. Greatly shocked she turned around and upon beholding her tormentor was about to reprimand him. He beat her to the punch, however, and assailed her elderly ears with a torrent of four letter words to the amusement of his adoring mother who stood talking to another woman nearby.

Indeed, in my time I have stood with ever-increasing disbelief while parents almost suffocated themselves with laughter at the awful sayings and dreadful doings of their own children. I am also aware of large numbers of parents who consider it great fun, entirely, when their offspring use a four-letter word. They even go so far as to insist that these toddling prodigies hold forth through the medium of effing and blinding for the benefit of friends, relations and other admirers who might happen to be in the vicinity. Over indulged by doting parents, the children exult in expressing themselves illicitly. Indeed, there is many a parent who believes that every foul utterance should be preserved for posterity.

Nobody can now deny that the use of the four letter word is at its most prevalent ever. When it was used in my boyhood days there was awe and shock. The user was branded as an authentic transgressor of the first water, bound to end his days with a rope around his neck and certain to sizzle, endlessly, on the scorching spits of hell!

This loathsome form of expressing oneself is also more prevalent among parents but I believe that this can be partially explained by the fact that it has now become too costly to smash, plates and saucers as a means of letting off steam. Banging doors is even more expensive because sooner or later a carpenter will have to be called in, while the cost of replacing broken windows has risen to astronomical proportions. The cheaper alternative is to avail of the four letter word. This might be, in view of what I have said, justifiable in itself provided no children are listening.

Expensive as is the banging of doors, the breaking of windows, the smashing of delph I would opt for these safety valves instead of the four letter ones. There is no satisfaction like the satisfaction that comes from a well banged door and no outlet for frustration so beneficial as the smashing of a dish, plate or saucer. Likewise the flinging of saucepans and pots here, there and everywhere is also a highly rewarding exercise. Effing and blinding, on the other hand, is not lasting and the treatment has to be repeated *ad nauseam*.

I was once witness to a row where the female of a partnership flung an alarm clock through her sitting-room window when her spouse arrived home with four of his cronies at one o'clock in the morning. Since I was one of the cronies aforementioned I had a frontline view of the proceedings. We arrived with two dozen bottles of stout and a span new deck of playing cards with a view to indulging in a spot of poker. All would have been well had not our host insisted that some rashers and sausages which happened to be in the fridge at the time should be fried on our behalf. As the contents of the pan sizzled there arose the unmistakable aroma of frying rashers. Whilst our entry and subsequent comings and goings in no way disturbed the woman of the house the smell of frying rashers quickly penetrated her slumber.

'Who's there?' she called harshly.

'Only us,' her husband responded foolishly.

'Who's us?' she demanded.

As he started to reel off the names of his companions ominous noises began from upstairs. Two of our number silently vanished. The rest of us stood idly by. Down the stairs she came with only her night-dress on and nothing in her hands save a well developed alarm clock.

'Out!' she screamed and with that she let fly with the alarm clock. It whirred harmlessly if speedily over our heads and crashed through the sitting-room window before landing on the street where it alarmed at great length and with distinction.

Some weeks later I met her on the street and apologised profusely for invading the privacy of her home at such an ungodly hour. She gladly accepted my apology and informed me in a dulcet voice that not an angry word had crossed her lips since the flinging of the alarm clock.

'I won't have to smash a thing now for months,' she explained which all goes to show that there are better ways of unleashing our frustrations than effing and blinding and a good alarm clock can be used year after year without any real damage to its structure.

Detail

Will you look at the details in Shakespeare's *Cymbeline:*

> *On her left breast*
> *A mole cinque-spotted, like the crimson drops*
> *I' the bottom of a cowslip.*

That's detail for you. Cinque is a word you'd rarely hear these days. There are, of course, the cinque ports these five havens on the southern shores of England – Hastings, Rommey, Hythe, Dover and Sandwich. At least I cinque so!

There is no detail like that of frost filigreed on winter window panes or the webs of spiders strung dew-bedecked on gorse and thorn in the morning light. Now there's detail beyond the capacity of human endeavour.

'Will you detail that for me,' demanded a retired schoolmaster one time after we had both applauded an extraordinary point during a game in the North Kerry Football Championship. He had set me an almost impossible task for, without doubt, it was one of the most magnificent points ever scored.

After receiving a ball, a precious and generous pass from a midfielder, the forward who had scored the point bent his head. He did not need to look at the goalposts for he already knew where he was. He side-stepped an opposing marker, sold a dummy to the centre halfback and then, restricted by the mandatory three steps of the time, drew back his leg and unleash- ed a mighty kick which dispatched the ball, regardless of wind prevailing, currents capricious or ground slip- pery, directly between the goalposts some fifty yards away.

When I was a boy I once noted the awful details of a drunken tramp's face. There were bristles on his jaw as long and as strong as pine needles and there was a purply hue to his bulbous nose which made me feel that it might explode at any moment. I was very young at the time and if there had not been several others with me I would never have mustered the courage to institute such a close inspection of his battered fea- tures. The face of that drunken tramp was a master- piece and it's a great shame, I have since felt, that so many artists opt for beauty instead of ugliness because real art espouses both and should depict both with the same commitment.

That face still fascinates me as it did my young companions of the time. They were enthralled and their unanimous exudations of disgust indicated pro- found appreciation, especially when he turned over on his side and presented his other profile. Here was an ear lacerated beyond repair. It wasn't a cauliflower ear. These are still whole at the end of the day but this ear had a chunk taken out of his lobe and its removal had been executed with a skill similar to that of the exper- ienced confectioner excavating a disc from a flattened mass of dough. Incisive molars, indeed, and practised too no doubt.

Drunk as he was and deep as was his slumber, he did not snore. Rather did he snort in much the same way as a ravenous horse extricating its head in momentary appreciation from a satchel of oats. Here was nature in the very raw and true detail on public display for all to see.

There were clusters of hair extending from his nostrils. His unwashed ears also played host to sizeable wisps which extended to curls at the end.

I was quite carried away by that old tramp's face. It certainly wasn't an evil face. There were still fine vestiges of humour deeply immersed in his over-all physiognomy.

Then, unexpectedly, he opened his eyes and blearily looked us up and down. Then like all tramps he looked beyond us, beyond the obvious really for it is here that danger lurks. We withdrew ready for instant flight but he seemed concerned rather then angry.

'Go to bed. Go to bed outa that the lot o' ye,' was all he said before resuming his sleep, a sleep now more profound and more content, the true sleep of the just since he had fully performed his duty by sending us all off to bed.

Standing Hairs

If anybody ever tells you that hair does not stand on the tops of heads don't believe it. Hair does stand on heads as sure as nails grow on toes and as sure as cats purr. The reason why it is not accepted as a positive fact is that we who have been affrighted have not seen the hairs stand. We can only feel them standing.

The hair has stood on my head twice all told. I did not see it stand for the good reason that I did not have a mirror in my possession at the time. In my youth quite a number of young men carried small hand mirrors in their pockets. Whenever an opportunity presented itself they would hold the mirror at a distance and rearrange their hair with pocket combs. It was common practice.

On the two occasions during which my hair stood on my head religious matters were involved. The first time I reckon I was about seven years of age. I had been commissioned by an elderly lady in the street to fetch a bottle of holy water from a large barrel which was always full to overflowing in the grounds of the local church.

I was given the princely sum of tuppence to fulfil the commission. If the poor woman had any sense she would not have paid me until the holy water was delivered.

I left the bottle lying under the protective stone of an archway and went off to purchase some sweets. I forgot about the bottle until that evening. On my way home I saw the old woman standing in her doorway, her hands folded and an expectant look on her face. At least I thought it was an expectant look. I located the bottle, dashed to the church but found that the gate was closed. I hurried to the river and filled the bottle with river water. I assuaged my conscience by telling myself that it would be wrong to disappoint the old woman. As I handed over the bottle a local Nosy Parker who happened to be chatting with the old woman at the time suggested it was tap water and not holy water.

'Are you prepared to swear,' said she, 'that you didn't get this out of a tap?'

'I am,' I answered truthfully.

'It doesn't matter anyway,' she said, 'because I can tell by the taste.'

At that time large numbers of women drank holy water for what ailed them rather than gin or vodka as they do now.

As she tasted the holy water the hairs stood on my head. She could make or break me. Fortunately she confirmed that it was indeed holy water and the hairs on my head reverted to their normal positions once more. It had been a narrow escape.

It was a good thing too that it happened because I never tried the same subterfuge again. The second time my hair stood on my head was during a mission in Listowel Parish Church.

It was a Sunday evening and I could have been no more than thirteen at the time. I had attended children's missions before but now I was being admitted to the real thing for the first time.

The church was packed to capacity with men of all shapes and sizes, men of all ages and politics, married men and single, rich and poor, ignorant and educated as the saying goes although you'll find as many ignorant men among the educated as you will among the uneducated. All evening the male parishioners, shrived and unshrived, had been converging on the church. I was informed afterwards that the attendances at such missions accounted for ninety-nine per cent of the parish's male population.

A hush fell on the mighty throng when the missioner appeared. After some preliminaries which included the singing of 'Faith of Our Fathers' and the recital of the Rosary he crossed himself and told us, although not in such terms to fasten our safety belts.

He opened gently and gradually built up steam until he came to the climax.

This consisted of an account of the awful lamentations made by those unfortunate souls who had been consigned to eternal damnation. So agonising and bloodcurdling was his description of the screeching, wailing, screaming and choking of hell's inmates that the hair stood on my head and stayed standing there for a full minute until his voice had subsided and we were all allowed to return to *terra firma*.

It was the most harrowing experience of my life. The hair has not stood on my head since.

Committees

As a veteran of a thousand or more committee meetings I feel it is only proper that I should pass on some of my experiences. I have lost count of the number of committees on which I have served. Mostly, fellow members are decent men and women but alas there are a few who make life miserable for the rest of us. The worst of these is your common or garden tale-carrier who takes away garbled versions of the many commendable observations and suggestions submitted by committee members in the heat of the moment.

I was once accosted in a public house by a gentleman of uncertain temper and challenged to defend myself because of such vile tale-twisting. I was taken completely by surprise since I was totally unaware of how I stood accused. It transpired after several nerve-racking moments that I was being charged with the passing of a derogatory remark about the man who had challenged me. Unfortunately for me he happened to have the same surname as a well-known author and lecturer whose name had come up during the course of a meeting attended by the tale-carrier. Somebody had asked if he might be deemed suitable for the delivering of a lecture during Writers' Week.

My opinion was asked and I recalled for the rest of the committee how some colleagues of mine had told me that they had fallen fast asleep during the course of one of his lectures and perhaps, a trifle sarcastically, drew the conclusion that he might be better suited to address a seminar for insomniacs.

When I was accosted in the public house I denied ever having uttered a single word, derogatory or otherwise, about my accoster. He was one of those individuals who cannot be mollified by words alone when his dander is up so I wisely decided to make myself scarce by the simple expedient of pointing out to him that his flop was open. Open flops are still anathema to all civilised peoples. When his bloodshot eyes were diverted downwards I made good my escape.

A few days later I encountered him outside a bookmaker's premises studying the results sheet in the front window. Up until the time he had accosted me with his outrageous accusation I had always found him to be a fairly agreeable chap except when his disposition was activated and subsequently aggravated by intoxication. Also in my favour was the fact that the results sheet showed him to be the backer of the two winners. He turned around gleefully and finding no one else in the vicinity he advised me of his good fortune.

'I've a double up,' he shouted.

I congratulated him and then when he recognised me his expression changed for the worse. I was subjected to a dark look. Quickly I explained my position as best I could before the euphoria of his win wore off.

Fair play to him, he accepted my explanation and apologised for his behaviour in the public house. Under no circumstances would he disclose the name of his informant.

'But he's a mischief-maker,' I told him, to which he answered that the man meant well and that also he was his friend.

'He is neither a friend to you or to me,' I pointed out but then the dark look appeared once more and I decided that I would not pursue the matter.

As a result, the tale-carrier escaped punishment and lived to lie another day.

Mary, Mary

My missus, that sainted woman who has persevered with me for thirty-five years, always maintains that she has never been called by her correct name. There is considerable substance to her claim.

She was born into this world Mary O'Connor. The O'Connor's are a proud people and it's no wonder she complains about not being properly addressed.

From the age of one month onwards she became known as Mary the Pensioner. Now how could she have been a pensioner, the intelligent reader (and there are many reading this piece) will ask.

The answer is that her grandfather served in the Boer War and when the war was over he was rewarded with a pension of tenpence a day which was a small fortune in 1902, which was the year the war ended. He could drink his fill and smoke his fill and have plenty left at the end of the day.

Time passed and my wife grew up into a fine cut of a girl. She was truly beautiful and was much admired not only in her own part of the world but wherever she went, into the bargain. When I first saw her I was totally smitten.

Now the people of the area and further afield came to the conclusion that to call such a girl a pensioner was a rank injustice and the upshot of the whole business was that she has not been called Mary the Pensioner for some time.

Instead she was called Mary the Shop and the

reason she was called Mary the Shop was because her people had a shop.

Curious people will inevitably ask why call the girl Mary the Shop when her real name is Mary O'Connor. Well the answer to that one is that people in that part of the world liked to put extra tags of identification on the people to avoid confusion. You see, dear reader, there might be as many as three other Mary O'Connors in a single townland whereas in the parish of Knocknagoshel alone there were at one particular reckoning as many as eleven Mary O'Connors.

Therefore, the extra tag was as necessary if not as exquisite as the subject which it adorned.

So for many years my wife was known as Mary the Shop. I never called her by such a prosaic name but rather by a whole variety of the most poetical and alluring nomenclatures. But while I would be expected, in view of our steady courtship, to provide such names, friends and neighbours and even strangers took it upon themselves to call her Mary the Shop.

Some older people still called her Mary the Pensioner but these were fading fast and the day would come when hardly anybody at all would call her by that name.

But let us press on. We have now deduced that my wife was provided unwittingly with two extra names up until the time of her marriage.

She foolishly believed that she would be called Mary Keane after she married and so she was for a while but it so happened that there were several other Mary Keanes in the parish of Listowel and in the surrounding countryside and it was not long at all before she was presented with her third and what I hopefully believe is her final name.

Now what do you think they called her when she came to Listowel. You'll never guess so I'd better tell you. They called her Mary John B.

'Imagine,' said a neighbour, 'saddling such a lovely woman with such an awful name.'

I don't agree at all because if she ever gets lost she'll have no bother finding her way home.

138

Cruelty to Greyhounds!

Three people were recently involved in a dispute on these here licensed premises. As well as being licensed to sell beer, wines, spirits and tobacco, we are also licensed to engage in non-violent disputes from time to time.

The subject of the most recent dispute was coursing, that kind of coursing where two dogs chase a hare with a view to tearing him asunder.

'Coursing is so cruel,' said a mild-mannered old lady as she made gentle conversation with two local coursing men, one of them her brother-in-law, the other a farmer.

'Coursing is cruel,' the latter agreed while the brother-in-law nodded his head emphatically.

'Do you remember that brindled bitch I had that could pick up a hare on the trot not to mind a gallop?' the farmer reminisced.

'Yerra why wouldn't I remember her,' said the brother-in-law, 'didn't the same lady win a bitch trial stake in Glin about twenty years ago.'

'But coursing is so cruel,' the old lady shook her head at the injustice of it all.

'Isn't that what we're after saying,' said her brother-in-law. 'Didn't this poor man have to put down that bitch after she breaking her two legs going after a hare. What could be crueller than that?'

The sister-in-law's mouth opened but she was obliged to open it again for the want of something appro-

139

priate to say. 'I had a black dog myself,' said the brother-in-law, 'that took a tumble in a no-course duffer in Clare and she broke her back. I had to shoot her. Don't talk to me about cruelty. I had another dog. She was a bitch and she rose a hare one day and we walking through a meadow at the back of the house. What did my hoor of a hare do only dodge under a fence of thorny wire and let my unfortunate dog run into it. He destroyed himself. He was never any good after that.'

'What about the hare?' said the sister-in-law, the astonishment showing clearly on her face.

'Don't mind the hare,' said the farmer, 'you'll see hares turning on children soon since they started doing away with all the coursing meetings. When the cat is out!'

'I can't understand why people go to coursing meetings at all,' said the old lady.

'Neither can I,' said her brother-in-law, 'there's no money in it and if you have a good dog you're risking his career if he meets a tough hare. It's not the gain that carries us to coursing but the pure love of it.'

The old lady sat holding her heart, unable to believe her ears.

'There's nothing crueller than coursing,' said the brother-in-law. 'I don't know why we follow it at all. A good coursing dog often broke his owner.'

'And his owner's heart,' his friend added.

'But!' the old lady protested, 'but what about the poor unfortunate hares. Look at what they have to go through.'

Her listeners looked at her in perplexity. It was the perplexity of the misunderstood.

'I often cursed hares,' said her brother-in-law, 'two

dogs and a bitch I lost over 'em. A dog will follow coursing rules but a hare, the hoor, won't!'

'That's right,' said his crony, 'a strong hare will destroy the best of dogs and there's no resorting to law.'

Both men shook their heads at the injustice of it all.

'You should never course a quality dog,' said the farmer. 'Safer to keep him for the track. That's where the money is. There's too much of a risk in coursing.'

'I'll tell you something now,' said the brother-in-law, and he laid a confidential hand on the old lady's shoulder. 'You take it from me that a game hare, a strong hare now, will do for the best of dogs. A greyhound has no chance at all against a game hare!'

Where Have All the Old Folk Gone?

There are no more old people and Amen say I to that and oh how women have changed, especially women who used to be called old!

Nowadays they drink gin and brandy and vodka and pints of beer, and they have every right to do so, but in my boyhood they used to be their own worst enemies.

When I was a garsún they wore sombre shawls and long coats and dumpy costumes. They never used make-up and why would they when it was condemned from the altar. Painting one's toes was the last of all and going off on a holiday was unheard of.

Didn't I hear them in my very own street when a woman walked in or out of a pub and how they would raise their eyes heavenwards whenever an unfortunate female passed by wearing trousers! Didn't I listen when a woman walked down the street in her figure which only meant that she was wearing a dress with no corset underneath.

'Oh the hussy!' they would say.

Secretly they longed for her gumption and disregard for convention. It would come in the course of time, a long time.

Women in their sixties, seventies and eighties now have their hair done regularly whereas in my boyhood they would be considered daft should they dare to have it done more than four times in the round of a year. These days they flirt and court and paint their nails, toes and fingers, and age has nothing to do with it. They have discovered that being old is purely and simply a state of mind.

How long since you heard anybody criticising a woman for drinking a pint of lager! for wearing a pair of trousers! for swearing or for staggering! For generations theses practices were confined to men.

In my boyhood the women who wore bikinis on the beaches and in their own back gardens suffered the hardest onslaughts of all. I even knew a girl who lost her job for wearing a bikini during a sultry weekend in Ballybunion. Even in my twenties if a woman walked into a public house on her own she would be the talk of the place. The only female who would dare walk with impunity on her own into a licensed premises would be a nun collecting the contributions from a donation box.

I haven't seen an old woman in a month of Sundays. Where, you may well ask, have they gone?

They have gone the way of haycars and ponycarts and long Sunday sermons, gone the way of black teeth and carbolic and castor oil and hairy bacon. They are gone the way of pannies and griddles and duck eggs, of suspenders, money balls and blackjack pipes, of hobnailed boots and haipneys and home-filled puddings, of flour dip and bloomers and potato cakes.

Will they ever return? Who is to say! All I know for sure is that these days you're as old as you feel and I can't say for sure whether this new trend is for the better or for the worse. I'm not ancient enough yet to know. I'm only sixty-three, on the threshold of a bright new future barring a fall or a bit of bad luck, another

The Ram of God and Other Stories

one of life's passengers dependent on God's will.

These days it's as good to be old as it is to be young, and isn't it high time the old came into their own. It's great to see them out and about and mixing with the young. They make great listeners and they fully understand the fears and worries of the young too whereas the young have yet to be old.

How To Go Without Staying

Give me the man who can travel without ever arriving. There's your true traveller. His journey is never over.

How often in my own travels have I been sorely disappointed on my arrival. It was for this reason, about five years ago, that I decided never to travel to anywhere again. I would travel, yes, but I would keep travelling. I would dispense with destinations, those awful pressurisers, which insist that we arrive at a certain place at a certain time.

Nowadays, I travel through places rather than to places. I tell myself when I am boarding a train to Dublin that I am merely availing myself of the city for one reason or another, whether to appear on television or attend a football match or whatever. It is with the city's amenities that I am concerning myself rather than with the city itself. I am therefore, a bird of passage.

The late and great Jack Faulkner, the travelling man, never travelled to any place.

Jack once came to me for a small loan.

'I am going as far as Puck,' said he, 'and I'll pay you as soon as I pass this way again.'

He paid me in the due course of time. Jack always paid. Notice that he said he was going 'as far as Puck', not 'to Puck'.

I pointed this out to him at the time.

'Ah you see,' said Jack, 'Puck is only a halt and you can't go to a halt. You pass through a halt after halting. All towns are only halts.'

He disclosed that, as soon as he had halted for awhile in Puck, he might move through Killarney for a day or two to have a look at the Yanks and the Lakes. After a look around Beauty's Home he would pass back through Tralee and thence to Listowel where he would pay me a visit and regale me with a colourful account of his travels.

After a few pints he would head for the only permanent home he had ever known in the town of Glin next door to his friend the Knight. You might therefore draw the conclusion that Jack was going to Glin because he had his home there but this wasn't the case at all.

Jack was going to Glin all right but he was going so that he could go through it and then through Foynes so that he could visit some old friends in Shanagolden. Therefore, he was not, strictly speaking, going to Glin specifically. He was going on the road.

To go anywhere is to tie yourself down. If you decide positively on going to a particular place, without leaving yourself any other option, you are incarcerating yourself and denying yourself the basic right to true freedom. Last evening I was in Ballybunion at the height of the storms. I walked the strand and listened to the thunder of the waves. I savoured the clear white of the great breakers and I became one with the elements. Then lest I be blown away I decided to vacate the beach and go home till the storm blew over.

On the road a man flagged me down and asked if I was going to Listowel.

'Sit in,' I told him, 'and I'll drive you to Listowel.'

'I don't want to put you out,' he said.

'Sit in,' I advised.

He sat in and we drove off but there was an uneasy silence. I decided not to break it. Why should I? He spoke after about two miles.

'I was not sure you'd be going to Listowel,' he said, 'but are you sure I'm not taking you out of your way?'

'You are not taking me out of my way,' I informed him, 'because I am going towards Listowel at this point in time and the fact that you desired to go there confirmed for me that I should indeed go to Listowel.'

'But you live there,' he said, as if that were sufficient reason.

'I know I live there,' I said, 'but that doesn't mean that I have to go there. Often,' I continued, 'while on my way in the direction of Listowel I have turned off at Gale Cross and taken the road to Finuge.'

It was apparent from his long, ensuing silence that he wasn't getting my drift and that he thought I was being clever.

'Look,' I said, 'just because I live in Listowel and happened to be going in the direction of Listowel when you flagged me did not mean that I was definitely going there. I never go places,' I went on.

'But you'll get to Listowel sometime,' he insisted.

'Of course, I will,' I told him, 'with the help of God.'

'And His holy Mother,' said he.

'And His holy Mother,' said I.

I did not bother to justify my situation further. Let him draw his own conclusions. When Jack Faulkner told me that he was not going to Puck but through Puck I knew exactly what he meant because I had been secretly contemplating the adoption of a similar dis-

147

position for years. I eventually did and discovered there were many new dimensions to life.

Let me put it another way. It was a wise man who said we only pass this way once. That is exactly what I am doing, passing this way once. I am going somewhere all right, in the end, but I am not sure where although I am hopeful that it is the place where I want to go.

All the time I am passing through so that I can eventually get there. I am certainly not in a hurry.

I go at my own pace, all the time passing through, although seeming to go to particular places. The fact is that I am going on only one journey and the rest of the places I will visit or sojourn, no matter for how long, are only halts or stopovers.

It gives me a wonderful sense of freedom to know that I no longer have to go anywhere. I can go around in circles or I can go back and forth because back and forth is all right. It's travelling.

This morning my wife said to me: 'You have to go to Dublin next week.'

'Read my next essay,' I told her, 'and you'll see whether I have to go or not.'

She took no notice. She is well used to my eccentricities by now or so she says.

Illusions of Grandeur

Boils, carbuncles, warts and the like which painfully present themselves from time to time on the faces of their unfortunate victims are always visible to the naked eye and might seem to be too much of a burden for the proprietors of these unwanted disfigurations but the fact is that they can be seen. Even if the sufferer does not look into mirrors some kindly relation or neighbour is sure to point them out and very often tender a successful cure.

It's different with those who suffer from illusions of grandeur because these delusions do not manifest themselves openly so that the onlooker cannot offer succour to the victims. Grandeur does not always manifest itself in the orthodox fashion but it is there to be seen if one is willing to perceive with true commitment. Alas it sometimes distorts the lives and outlooks of those who suffer from it and it sometimes distorts the lives and outlooks of family and friends.

Take the case of Micky Pit. Pit was a nickname. Micky was a highly successful small farmer who subsisted chiefly on the income from the milk of nine cows and a modest vegetable garden. His soil was not really suited to the growth of potatoes but this, alas, was no deterrent to Micky. He was advised time after time by established potato growers that he would be better off trying to grow some other crop. Micky would have none of it. Every year he planted a large garden of potatoes.

The crop was always small and the return on his investment was practically nil. Then came a disastrous year and Micky's potato crop was at an all time low. Micky would not give it to say that he had been wrong and his neighbours right so he built a huge earthen potato pit in his haggard and in it placed his crop. It dwarfed all the other pits in the neighbourhood.

Micky fooled nobody. In a short time he ran out of spuds and but for the kindness of his in-laws his family would have starved.

The years passed and it turned out that people forgot his real surname and began to call him Micky Pit. That was bad enough but whenever a man would tell an outrageous story about his possessions or his achievements in the local public house the other customers would say: 'He's like Micky Pit's haggard, all pit and no spuds.'

And what about the grand woman of the three cows maligned in the immortal poem: 'Oh Woman of Three Cows!':

> *Oh woman of three cows agraw*
> *Don't let your tongue thus rattle,*
> *Don't be sauncy, don't be proud,*
> *Because you may have cattle.*
> *Grand woman here's my hand to you*
> *That what I say is true,*
> *There's many a man with twice your stock*
> *Not half as proud as you.*

I have never agreed with the sentiments expressed in this poem and this woman differs from Micky Pit in spite of what the poet says. It was clear that she was, in fact, in possession of the aforementioned three cows and if she boasted itself it has to be remembered that they were her own cows.

A little boasting is no great harm now and then especially if there's nobody around to sing the praises of the party who has something to boast about. The woman of three cows, for instance, never said that she had six cows. She only boasted about the three to which she had legitimate claim and it could well be that the poet who wrote so cruelly of her was maybe a man with no cow at all.

The woman's fault was that she wasn't cute. If she had waited there can be no doubt that some well-disposed, detached cow-critic would eventually pass the way and heap upon the cows the encomiums they deserved.

There was another factor which the poet who wrote so derogatorily might have taken into account if he was a generous observer of the human scene. It is possible that the woman may have been planning the sale of one or all the cows in order to pay the rent. If a person is selling off cattle one does not run them down. One must praise them if one is to get the best price. I, therefore, must come to the conclusion that the poet was an envious neighbour who, if he had his own cows for sale, would have praised them to the very moon.

We see then how there are instances of justifiable grandeur as well as grandeur which can be destructive. *Quod semper, quod ubique, quod ab omnibus!*

An Unfortunate Leak

Story peddling is my vocation. I can write about anything as distinct from the story carrier who is pretty choosy about the quality of the merchandise he elects to transport. Under no circumstances will he burden himself with stories that might be in the least bit edifying.

For instance, suppose some neighbour were to win a prize in a lottery or achieve something spectacular in some other sphere, they would rather wait until these individuals committed some indiscretion which was more worthy of their notice and, as a consequence, worthy of transportation to other outlets who delight in the distribution of evil tidings free of charge.

A friend of mine, a most exemplary fellow who managed to struggle through life without exposing his weaknesses was, alas, brought to book a short while ago. Never mind the fact that he had reared a highly successful and happy family by foregoing all manner of luxuries while they were growing up. He was ably assisted by his wife who worked like a slave for family and home.

Anyway after he had reared his clutch he found himself with money go leor and as soon as he saw to his wife's needs he took to frequenting public houses where the poor fellow drank his fill. Some of his neighbours said that he drank too much and one night, one awful night, his critics were vindicated.

His relief expedition, for such it was as shall be

seen, was observed by a neighbour and that was that! All he did, poor fellow, was to leave the main thoroughfare because he failed to locate a public toilet thereon; neither could he find a public house where he might avail himself of the facilities which all decent hostelries boast.

He proceeded along a side street until he came to the premises of a pharmaceutical chemist. The shop boasted two large front windows. One of these displayed a new and comprehensive line of toilet accessories but while he had no difficulty distinguishing the word toilet he was baffled by the word accessories, which appeared in much smaller print. He piddled against the window with serenity and confidence.

The unfortunate man was the talk of the community for several days thanks to the communicative powers of his neighbours, not one of whom was prepared to make excuses for him.

Then something else happened and our friend's indiscretion faded into the background. I forget what it was that took the spotlight away from him but it cannot have been much or I would be able to recall it.

In my time I have been reluctantly obliged to listen to hundreds of tales about my neighbours. Many of them may well have been true. Knowing the human species it must be said that they are capable of anything.

It is, as the old woman said when she was being swept away by the flood, only all going through life!

How right she was, for no matter what indiscretions we may commit they are merely drops in the vast confluence of human folly which accumulates wherever there is an abundance of human life.

The moral here, of course, is that we must always

weigh the character of the detractor against the character of the victim when it will be plainly revealed that the latter always outweighs the former.

Foul Deeds Will Rise

There's many an honest Irish man and woman down on their knees thanking God for the arrival of the funeral parlour. Where once there was none now there are many.

How deprived now are those hawk-eyed inspectors of the indoor scene who looked upon a death in a neighbour's house as a passport to an uncharted land where new vistas might be examined and the manners and means of the inhabitants taken into account. These avid inquisitors would arrive at the scene before the off and take up their places at the bedside from which vantage point they were at liberty to study the hats, clothes, shoes and general appearances of every mourner who knelt by the deathbed to pray.

I often criticised them and now I'm sorry because I miss them more than I can say. They were part and parcel of the rural scene and they kept us all on our toes. With two rows of these redoubtable matrons ranged at either side of the bed, their hands decorated with massive dangling rosaries, there was no time for frivolity and the corpse was accorded his fair modicum of respect.

Once I was present in a wake-room when a sacrilegious act was perpetrated. I was on my knees at the time and so were the others, a fat man who smelled of freshly consumed whiskey and two women whose bodies and visages were covered by black shawls which were in common use at the time. As we were being relentlessly vetted there was an eerie silence which was common only to wake rooms. Suddenly it was broken by a sharp succession of poorly suppressed wind breakages.

The sounds died as quickly as they had come, leaving behind a silence far more devastating than the first. Then came a gasp of horror and outrage from the several females in attendance. It was unequivocal in its condemnation. The kneeling females shook their heads and gazed with sorrow at the fat man who continued with his praying as though no such earth-shaking and sacrilegious outrage had taken place.

He rose, blessed himself, and withdrew to the porter room which was the name given to that area where the alcoholic beverages were being distributed.

He was followed by one of the two women who knelt by my side. Deeply scandalised by the unexpected outburst she retired meekly to the kitchen where tea was being served.

The other woman was next to rise. I slunk out after her but as she exited from the room, just out of earshot of the inquisitors, she unleashed a minor tattoo from the rear, similar in all respects to those to which we had been subjected in the wake-room.

How right was Shakespeare:

Foul deeds will rise
Though all the earth o'erwhelm them to men's eyes.

Letter from a Left Foot

Recently I saw a footballer drive a penalty wide. He was left-footed. Having managed to avoid the net he bent and upbraided his left leg and also the shoe which encased it.

Here now is a letter written by the left leg to the brain of the man who kicked the ball wide.

Dear Master,

I am reminding you of the game against Kilduvve. A sunnier, milder Sunday was never sponsored by the heavens. What a carnival spirit there was to dilute the heart-spurring tension! The world and his wife were at the game.

Alas before the final whistle was blown on that awful occasion it was I, your left foot, who was pilloried, persecuted and impeached. It was I who was made to pay for your continuing caprices and for your all too characteristic lapses in commitment.

None of your other limbs or organs have ever suffered such a moment of degradation as this.

The warning signs had been present for weeks beforehand. How often during training did I protest about the curtailment of toe movement, the constriction of instep, the murderous marasmus of ankle, heel, shinbone and ligament, the frustration and obstruction of arteries and the all-round numbness caused by the tight-fitting football boot which you steadfastly refused to replace.

You might easily have had it comfortably enlarged for less than the price of a single beer but no, you parsimonious wretch, you preferred to proceed with the beleaguerment of your already bursting bladder.

How I loathed you on that ignominious afternoon as you strutted like a gamecock with your chest expanded to the penalty area as though the scoring of the goal was a foregone conclusion.

I recalled the countless, fruitless signals which I had dispatched to you during the long weeks of training. I conveyed my pain and discomfort to you as effectively as I could.

You acknowledged me all right for I noted you grimace when a pang with a particular sting was communicated to you.

I heard your mouth cry out with pain whenever you leaned on my long-suffering sole and still you refused to take the action which would render me one hundred per cent mobile and transform me into the deadly shooting machine which training and skill have long ordained that I should be. You sir are a brain which cannot see beyond your nose.

The red blood righteously surges to the very tips of my badly compressed toes as though it would haemorrhage through skin and nail when I recall how you acknowledged the unmerited plaudits of the adoring crowd as you lifted the leather lamprey-like on to a single palm.

Then having felt and weighed it in both hands you placed it carelessly on the penalty spot from where all present presumed, your good left foot excepted, you would consign it deftly and effortlessly to the back of the net.

You stood cool as a breeze unfettered and unconfined whilst I furiously transmitted SOS after SOS in the forlorn hope that you might at least loosen the lace that confined me and thus restore my full firing power before you bore down upon the ball.

O vainglorious muff! Oh duffer without peer! Oh blundering, lumbering apology for a penalty-taker!

No. You should ignore my every entreaty and assume the classic pose of a Pele or a Maradonna with hands placed casually on hips and slack cranium slightly to one side as though the immediate execution of a penalty was the last thought in your head.

Thus you stood totally impervious to my now demented supplications. When I felt your other limbs assemble and stiffen as they awaited your command I too readied myself and dismissed as best I could my terrible discomfort. I rallied with the others in a do-or-die effort to save an impossible situation. I would do my utmost in the last desperate moments.

You moved. I flexed myself. You reached the ball. You drew me back too hastily, too gingerly and you kicked prematurely. There was only one way the ball could have gone and that was wide.

Bad as that was, your next act was the most heinous of all. You bent and reviled my good self and the unfortunate boot I was wearing. Oh the shame! Oh the degradation! Oh the perfidy as you walked with your head held high away from the goal, as though you were guiltless of the vile crime which you had carelessly perpetrated.

Yours sincerely,
Your Left Foot

A Useful Man

'The road will shape you into a useful man'. When I first heard the expression I already believed I was a useful man so that I resented being told so. The man who made the observation was a neighbouring trades-man who had seen his share of the world over a life-time and of course I should have listened. I was young however and could not be expected to listen for like most young folk I already knew everything.

I was on my way to England at the time. It would have been the night before my first crossing. A group of us were seated in the local pub. A friend was leaving the country with me. He was the same age as I was which meant that he had no experience either.

The man who told me that the road would shape me into a useful man was dead right. For all my years, a grand total of twenty-one, I was dependent on many people and would continue to be dependent on many people before it could be said that I was a useful man. There are many who never become useful men. They just aren't up to it or they aren't made that way. The intervention and aid of others is required from time to time to ensure that they are not submerged in the floods of struggle and strife.

Then there are the fortunate few who are born into this world without corners. For them life can be easy unless tragedy strikes. The bother is that tragedy gives no warning.

Still he is thrice blessed who has no corners for he

need never undergo the horrors of having the corners knocked off him. The man with whom I was travelling to England had no corners at all except that he would not or could not eat fat meat and because of this his mother would often upbraid him. He never took any notice even when she pointed out to him that a pig or a cow or a sheep had yet to be born without fat.

In England because he had no corners the landlady quickly deduced that he was not a lover of fat meat and always saw to it therefore that there was no fat meat on his plate. This wasn't always easy because meat was rationed at the time in England. While the man with no corners sailed blithely through the shoals and eddies of life I, who was his friend, was having corners knocked me every day so that it should have been said that I was shaping into a useful man.

The trouble with me was that no sooner was one corner demolished than another started to be rebuilt in its place. It was much the same as the old theory of the fly in the ointment. There is, it is universally agreed, a fly in every ointment. Since you cannot squash flies on ointment without destroying the ointment you must wait until the fly succeeds in releasing himself. Failing that the fly must be extricated skilfully so that the mixing of the ointment can be completed. Here is where the trouble arises. For every fly in every ointment there are hundreds of others in the vicinity, all awaiting the chance to replace the resident fly. Our ointments are therefore never without flies.

It is the same with me and with corners. For every corner that has been painfully removed over the years, nay, the generations, there have been others waiting in the wings to take their places.

My friend who had no corners had an easy life.

You would never catch him in an argument although he drank as much as everybody else. He was blessed with a gentle and benign disposition while we, his companions, were suspicious and cautious and ready to fly off the handle at the drop of a hat. While my friend who told me that the road would shape me into a useful man was right in many respects he was wrong in as many others. Even when corners stop growing because the proprietor is too old there are still many derelict corners left on his human outlook. These corners of the mind cannot be ever totally removed. The secret is to accept yourself, corners and all, and other people will come to accept you as well.

I don't altogether trust a man without corners but that could well be because I envy him. The moral here is know your corners and you will begin to know yourself. How's that Shakespeare puts it:

> *... to thine own self be true,*
> *And it must follow, as the night the day,*
> *Thou canst not then be false to any man.*

Isn't that exactly what I was saying. Know your own corners and you'll know every other corner. It's not the first time that Shakespeare borrowed a line or two from me. His mother was from Kerry or so I am told, born not far from the village of Tarbert which nestles so peacefully on the Shannon estuary.

However let us return to the shaping of men. The road I am prepared to concede, plays a big hand in it and since God never puts old heads on young shoulders our youth will have to suffer during the shaping. But where's the point the cynic will ask. As soon as a man is shaped he is ready to be measured for his shroud so the question might well be asked are we merely being shaped into useful men so that we can die useful rather than live useful men. No. No. No. What happens is this. We are shaped into useful men so that we may savour life in our later years and direct our young in the vain hope that they will not make the same mistakes that we made. We are also shaped so that we have the time and the contriteness to atone for our sins. But why all this philosophising about morbid themes the reader will ask!

Very simple. This evening I had bacon and turnips for dinner and whenever I over-indulge in turnips I have a most morose outlook for at least twenty-four hours. Turnips also disagree with my digestive tract. Indeed there is another moral here. Say the time is around three o'clock in the afternoon. You enter a drapery to buy a shirt and the assistant is anti-you, even impertinent, gives you guff and, generally speaking, is unhelpful. The moral is to make an allowance always because he may be, like me, after a feed of turnips.

I'm not saying that we should blame turnips all the time but we should take them into consideration.

What was that the theme of our treatise was? Ah yes! The road will shape you into a useful man. That should read 'the road should shape you' not 'will shape you'.

I am forced to conclude that the road could also shape you into an idiot. Too much road like too much anything else is bad for both your body and soul whereas the home cements relationships and deepens our affection for each other after brief excursions elsewhere.

The Colour of Kerry

I could introduce the Kingdom of Kerry with a description of its incomparable physical attributes from Cahirciveen to Ballybunion but a few well-taken photographs would eclipse my most passionate prosopography.

I might also write about Kerry football and outline for you a particularly well-taken point from boot to crossbar but I would much prefer to write about the living lingo of the greater, hard-necked, Atlantical warbler known as the Kerryman who quests individually and in flocks for all forms of diversion and is to be found, high and low, winter and summer, wherever there is the remotest prospect of drink, sex, confusion or commotion!

Plain, everyday language is of no use to your genuine Kerryman. I remember to have been involved only last year in the purchase of a trailer of turf for my winter fires. A countryman friend, in order to bring down the price, spoke disparagingly of the trailer's size. Said he, dismissively, 'A young blackbird would bring more in its beak'.

On another occasion the same gentleman was breakfasting with some friends on the morning of an All-Ireland final. The fare consisted of the usual rashers, egg and sausage but, alas, the rashers were of the fatty variety and were possessed of no meat whatsoever. He put the rashers on his side plate and proceeded with the demolition of sausages and egg.

'Why,' asked the companion at the opposite end of the table, 'are you not eating your rashers?'

'Because,' said our friend, 'they are too fat.'

'Is there any taste of lean meat at all in them?' asked the other.

'No,' said our friend, 'not as much as you'd draw with a single stroke of a red biro!'

However, for all his wanton but worthwhile diffuseness our friend would regard himself as a rather inferior sort of Kerryman. 'A bit of a country boy', as he says himself. He reminds me of the Kerryman who thought he had an inferiority complex: 'I am only the same as everybody else,' said he.

There is no such entity as a conventional Kerryman. If you try to analyse him he changes his pace in order to generate confusion. He will not be pinned down and you have as much chance of getting a straight answer out of him as you would a goose egg out of an Arctic tern.

He loves words, however, and that's the only way you'll get him going. Snare him with well-chosen words and craftily-calefacted phrases and he will respond with sempiternal sentences, sonorous and even supernatural.

On the other hand, he also has the capacity for long, perplexing silences. It is when he seems to be speechless, however, that he is at his most dangerous. He is weighing up the opposition, waiting for an opening, so that he can demoralise you.

He never talks in ordinary terms and why should he when he can aspire otherwise?

Once, on our way back from a football game in Dublin a party of us stopped at a pub in West Limerick but we were refused admission on the grounds that there was more morning than night in the hour that was in it.

'Be not forgetful,' said the oldest of our party, remembering Saint Paul, 'to entertain strangers for thereby some have entertained angels unawares!'

'Let them in don't we be damned,' said the woman of the house who happened to be a Kerrywoman too.

An old man once told me that Kerrymen were uniquely articulate because the elements were their mentors.

'They can patter like rain,' said he, 'roar like thunder, foam like the sea, sting like the frost, sigh like the wind and on top of all that you'll never catch them boasting.'

More Interesting Titles

DURANGO

John B. Keane

Danny Binge peered into the distance and slowly spelled out the letters inscribed on a great sign in glaring red capitals:

'DURANGO,' he read

'That is our destination,' the Rector informed his friend. 'I'm well known here. These people are my friends and before the night is over they shall be your friends too.'

The friends in question are the Carabim girls: Dell, aged seventy-one and her younger sister, seventy-year-old Lily. Generous, impulsive and warm-hearted, they wine, dine and entertain able-bodied country boys free of charge – they will have nothing to do with the young men of the town or indeed any town ...

Durango is an adventure story about life in rural Ireland during the Second World War. It is a story set in an Ireland that is fast dying but John B. Keane, with his wonderful skill and humour, brings it to life, rekindling in the reader memories of a time never to be quite forgotten ...

LOVE BITES and other stories

John B. Keane

John B. introduces us to 'Corner Boys', 'Window Peepers', 'Human Gooseberries', 'Fortune-Tellers', 'Funeral Lovers', 'Female Corpses', 'The Girls who came with the Band' and many more fascinating characters.

MORE IRISH SHORT STORIES

John B. Keane

In this excellent collection of *More Irish Short Stories* John B. Keane is as entertaining as ever with his humorous insights into the lives of his fellow countrymen. Few will be able to resist a chuckle at the innocence of bachelor Willie Ramley seeking a 'Guaranteed Pure' bride in Ireland; the pre-occupations of the corpse dresser Dousie O'Dea who felt that 'her life's work was complete. For one man she had brought the dead to life. For this, in itself, she would be remembered beyond the grave'; at the concern of Timmy Binn and his friends for 'the custom to exhaust every other topic before asking the reason behind any visit': the intriguing birth of Fred Rimble and 'the man who killed the best friend'.

LETTERS OF A MATCHMAKER

John B. Keane

The letters of a country matchmaker faithfully recorded by John B. Keane, whose knowledge of matchmaking is second to none.

In these letters is revealed the unquenchable, insatiable longing that smoulders unseen under the mute, impassive faces of our bachelor brethren.

Comparisons may be odious but readers will find it fascinating to contrast the Irish matchmaking system with that of the 'Cumangettum Love Parlour' in Philadelphia. They will meet many unique characters from the Judas Jennies of New York to Fionnula Crust of Coomasahara who buried two giant-sized, sexless husbands but eventually found happiness with a pint-sized jockey from North Cork